Please
don't die

To anyone who has lost their person.

sands press
Brockville, Ontario

Please don't die

A Novel by Meghan Schiereck

sands press

sands press

A Division of 3244601 Canada Inc.
300 Central Avenue West
Brockville, Ontario
K6V 5V2

Toll Free 1-800-563-0911 or 613-345-2687
http://www.sandspress.com

ISBN 978-1-990066-26-9

Publisher's Note

This book is a work of fiction. References to real people, events, establishments, organizations, or locales, are intended only to provide as a sense of authenticity, and are used fictitiously. All other characters, and all incidents and dialogue, are drawn from the authors' imaginations and are not to be construed as real.

For information on bulk purchases of this book or any book published by Sands Press, please call 1-800-563-0911.

To book an author for your live event, please call: 1-800-563-0911

Sands Press is a literary publisher interested in new and established authors wishing to develop and market their product. For more information please visit our website at www.sandspress.com.

Chapter 1

I tape up the last box, and dust off my hands. *It's time to go.*

I feel it begin to boil up inside me again, like someone turned the stove burner under my stomach on high. I'm no stranger to this feeling. It's something I've felt every day—to every now-and-then—and every variation in between. I ignore it and pretend no one is home. It would leave in a moment just as fleeting as it came.

I'm not one to be good with explanations, especially with ones on things that never really had explanations. I still ask myself what it's like after all this time. There is no real reason for its arrival or its departure.

There's a privilege in parting, after all.

It's driving in a NASCAR race on an ancient, rickety bicycle.

It's getting kicked in the face by every happy family to ever live in the United States. It's a house fire that destroys your great-aunt's heirloom scarf collection.

It's a god-awful car accident that ruins your body and breaks all of your teeny, tiny fragile bones. It's your parents getting older. It's the end of your favorite show.

It's admitting your addiction, your alcoholism, and all of your sins to your horribly frail grandmother. It's finding out a family secret you were never meant to know.

You want to shred it like an old credit card statement. You want to stuff it into a ball and eat it like a meatball over some spaghetti.

You want to kick it in its ugly fucking face so hard that it needs plastic surgery to ever have a normal looking nose.

It laughs at you and all of your insecurities and your biggest failures and at anything that makes you smile. It says, "Look, you dummy! I'm going to make you cry over a pet food commercial!"

But soon enough, the constant heckling becomes as familiar as the dull rumble of the refrigerator, the howl of the neighborhood train horns and the pitter patter of big raindrops on your window.

You wander towering mountain ranges and windswept moors in search of escape to no avail. You are a malnourished, drenched orphan girl with no home and no dowry.

It has no shame in its bitter reminder, wearing it proudly like a first-place ribbon.

For weeks, making a phone call will be like pressing the doomsday button. Getting dressed will be like manslaughter. Leaving the house will be like drowning in six inches of water in your own bathtub. Doing anything will be like burning yourself alive as entertainment for a 16th century king. It makes you a hardened, shriveled shell of a person.

But it's also your best friend. It's your security blanket. It becomes your only comfort in this vast and evil world. You carry it everywhere you go. You are the Stockholm-syndromed prisoner, and you couldn't be happier.

It's a loving caress that—this is all over; it's done with; it's far in the past now. It's the only silver lining in this whole mess. It was natural causes, after all. This feeling is your comfort blanket in this cold, dark existence. It assures you that "Yes, sweetheart, he wasn't hurting."

One minute you were drinking coffee, waking up in the sunshine, and not minding your underpaid job. The next minute, you're watching a tear fall off his mother's nose, listening to her say, "I'm sorry sweetheart. His body just couldn't handle it. He was unconscious, and they couldn't get him back. He loved you—you know that, right?" *Right.*

You have to tell every person you see whether you want to or not. Your therapist. Your boss. Your neighbor. The banker. The convenience store cashier. The first date you go on after. Everyone must know about the life you were supposed to have, and now don't.

Through no volition of your own, you say to them, "My boyfriend died. We were going to get married. Do you want to see the memorial collage I made?" Repeat for the next three un-fucking-bearable years.

Grief. That motherfucker comes back every single time.

Especially when I'm leaving the only apartment I've ever known in New York City and the last place I'd seen Gio alive three years ago—that wasn't a sterilized hospital room. I hadn't wanted to move but I couldn't keep up with the rent hikes, and I couldn't stomach seeing a roommate seeing my carefully arranged Ziploc bags full of Gio's clothes, or the trail of snot-filled tissues that appeared every now and then, or the now extremely pitiful memorial collage I couldn't bear to take down.

So, moving it is. I won't be going far. Just a one-bedroom unit a few floors down. But it's not the two-bedroom with a fireplace and outdoor terrace I picked out with Gio a few years ago. I've had to really hype myself up for this move and convince myself I'm ready. I have to be. My wallet certainly is. I don't have a choice.

I'll miss this place. Gio and I moved here right after college. I made my very first painting commission here. Gio built our kitchen table to fit perfectly in the eat-in kitchen. It won't fit quite as well in the new apartment, but I'll still take it with me. I walked in as half of a whole, and I'll leave as whatever crumbs of my old self are left. Part of me is glad to go. I think, deep down, I knew I needed to start fresh somewhere, even if I wouldn't outwardly admit I wanted to. My therapist has slowly been encouraging me to say it was okay to move. It has to be.

Gio had a seizure a year after we moved in, and his glioblastoma diagnosis, a usually deadly brain cancer, was three weeks after that. He lived for ten months. I had lived alone in this apartment without Gio longer than he ever even imagined being here. It was more my apartment than it ever was his, but still, I couldn't help but think of it as ours. His name was on the initial lease, after all.

I hoist the box up onto my hip and collect my keys from the island countertop. I walk toward the door and scuff my feet on the floorboards one last time. *Goodbye, Apartment 504. See you never.*

I make my way down the hall to the elevator thinking that I'll drop off this last box at my new apartment then go downstairs to the building superintendent's office to return the old keys. As I reach to push the down button, the doors slide open and inside are two men carrying a brown, leather sofa. Trying to carry it, anyway. I guess it's moving day for someone else, too.

"I told you we should have hired movers," one says. He's slightly shorter than the other man, with pasty, acne-scarred skin, curly blonde hair, a wispy mustache and both arms covered in tattoos. He's dressed in a Def Leppard shirt, cargo shorts with red Converse and looks like he could be pulled from just about any Midwestern basement concert. Perfect for maneuvering a sofa. I can almost hear the sweat in his voice.

His companion, not so much. He's wearing what looks to be a chef's uniform. I don't know. It's been so long since I've been to a restaurant that had actual chefs. The Red Kettle is embroidered on the top right of the jacket, with a teeny-tiny design of a red kettle with steam billowing out.

"Shut up," says Chef. "Just get out of the elevator." He is taller than the pasty guy and his shiny black hair flops to one side and falls in his face while he strains to carry the sofa. Neither of them move out of the elevator.

"I'm trying!" exclaims Pasty Boy, who keeps turning his head to see where he can back out.

"Hurry up, I can't hold this much longer!" Chef exclaims back. "What's your problem?"

I step away to the side and clear my throat as if to say, "Okay, you can get out of the elevator now." I do not want to talk to these two. I want to get downstairs, drop off my box, get rid of these godforsaken keys and binge watch *New Girl* for the twentieth time. I should have taken the stairs.

"My hands are clammy. Give me a second, Jordan!" Pasty boy answers, taking a step into the hallway as soon as the elevator doors begin to close, after what seems like a century. The stairs are looking like the best option.

Jordan forges forward, pushing Pasty along. I walk backwards as they maneuver the couch out. Have they not even noticed me? They keep coming and soon I'm cornered against the wall. They must have noticed me. I try to get around, but the couch is blocking any exit route I could possibly take. Pasty drops the couch with a solid thud as soon as they are out of the elevator. They've seen me.

"Murphy, I swear to God. I have to be back at 4:00. Pick up the couch," Jordan says.

"Hello there, might you know where apartment 504 is?" Murphy asks. I stare back blankly. He's clearly asking me.

Fuck. They sure didn't waste any time getting a new tenant. How are they even going to get in? I have the keys! Jordan rolls his eyes faster than I can roll mine. Murphy just wipes his hands on his shorts.

"It's that way." Jordan and I both answer at the same time. I point down the hall from whence I came. I dangle the keys.

"I have the keys though. I was the previous tenant. You won't be able to get in."

"Oh, well, could you just give them to us?" Jordan asks, his lips pursed, clearly hoping for a possible shortcut.

It's 3:45 already. His ill-preparedness is not my fault. I don't feel comfortable not returning the keys directly to the super. What if these two clowns don't really live here?

"I don't know..." I stammer. "I'm supposed to return them. I really don't feel comfortable giving them to a stranger."

"You live here, right? I'm not a stranger. I'm your neighbor. I'm Jordan Park, apartment 504." Jordan gives me a small grimace and holds his hands out for the keys.

"I think I'd just prefer to give them to the super. The office is just in the lobby. They're expecting me." I attempt to make my way around the couch to get to the staircase. It's just five flights down.

Murphy cracks his back and yawns. "It's fine, Jordan, I'll just wait here with the couch. Why don't you go down with her?"

"I don't have time. I have to start dinner prep at 4:00! The dinner service starts at 5:30. It's 3:45. I'm wasting time just standing here!" He pushes his thumb and index finger between his eyebrows. "Could you just give us the keys? I will explain to the super what happened." Jordan is getting frustrated, if not at me, at his mover.

"I'm sorry. I would really just rather follow the proper move-out directions. I really need my security deposit back." I am getting stressed. Jordan is clearly pressed for time and growing increasingly more frustrated with Murphy, who has now sat down on the sofa.

"Please." He almost begs me while I attempt to climb over the couch to reach the stairs without much success. I don't think I can make it over without stepping on it and Murphy is now clearly browsing Instagram. *Fuck it, I'm so pissed I could cry. They've backed me into a literal corner.*

I hoist myself up and over the back of the couch, my red sneakers leaving a dirty footprint on the cushion.

"Hey! Don't put your feet on my furniture!" Jordan snaps.

"Maybe don't leave your furniture blocking residents in!" I snap back.

"Maybe you had given us the keys, we'd have been out of your way minutes ago!"

"Maybe you should schedule your time better!" I'm embarrassed for arguing with a stranger in the hallway who is now moving into my beloved apartment. I harshly push open the stairwell door and stomp my way down. "I'll write you a check for a dry cleaner or whatever."

"Hey! You!" Jordan shouts after me. "Just give me the keys!"

I don't answer and keep descending. Jordan is just a few paces behind me. Surely he will catch up. I don't want to see the man who will be living in my home. I don't want anything to do with him. I feel tears welling up in my eyes, catching in my eyelashes, blurring my vision.

"What's your problem? Why are you being such an asshole? It's just a key!"

Am I being an asshole? No. I have hardly said five sentences to the man. Sure, I want to follow proper procedure and not cut corners. That hardly makes me an asshole. "If you're having a bad day, don't take it out on me!"

But stepping on his furniture *did* make me an asshole. I was the asshole. All I wanted was to get into my new apartment and pretend this day was over. I don't want to explain that I'm being an asshole because my fiancé is dead, and now I can't afford my dream apartment—that he's moving into. I doubt he has the patience to understand why I'd be such an asshole on a day like this, and I don't want to give him the explanation.

I burst into the lobby and round the corner to the super's office.

"I'm sorry, just—"

I'm so exasperated I fling the door open and throw the keys onto the super's desk. They skitter across the surface and onto the floor.

"There's your keys," I choke out. Someone has thrown a stake in a sandbag in my lungs and I feel like I can't breathe. The realization that someone who isn't me is going to be living in my apartment is hitting me. *Our apartment.* No one should be living there but me and Gio.

Big, fat cartoon tears drip down my cheeks and I one hundred percent guarantee I look like a fucking maniac over a set of keys. I take a huge gulp of air and try to regain my composure.

The super sits there mildly stunned, as all of our previous interactions consisted of pleasantly quiet hellos at the mailboxes or awkward shuffles in the garbage alley.

"I'm sorry about the keys. I'm in a hurry."

I need to get out of this office, and to calm down, but Jordan blocks the doorway. I can not start grieving the apartment right here, even though my body clearly has other plans.

It's just an apartment. I try to calm myself. "Can you move please?" I ask Jordan. "I have somewhere I need to be." *Wrapped in my weighted blanket, holding my dog, and wishing I was reborn as literally anyone else in my next life.*

"Do you let all your tenants throw keys at you?" Jordan asks the super, with a sardonic tone in his voice.

"Not usually, no," the super answers.

"Again, I apologize. I won't be any more trouble. Please, can you move?" My eyes begin to water. *Not again, please. I can handle moving out.*

Jordan begins to shift to the side before he suddenly reaches to grab my shoulder as I'm leaving. I step just outside of his grasp, irritated he thinks he can touch me.

"Don't step on my couch again." He looks me straight in the eye. His eyes are almond shaped with deep, dark brown irises, and a smattering of freckles cross his nose. There's a hint of a smile on his face, as if he finds my hysterical behavior over the keys amusing.

"Don't leave your couch in the hall." I snap angrily, pull the door shut, and head towards the elevator. I make it five paces before the tears start flowing freely.

Floor 3. Apartment 321. My new home awaits me. Petunia, my aging Boston terrier, is probably snuggled tightly on our own couch. She was a present to Gio after his diagnosis, in an attempt to help solidify our rocky future. I doubt she even remembers him.

As I fish for my new keys in my pocket, I think to myself about one of the very first grief group therapy sessions I attended. They said, "Go where the memories are."

When someone dies, you should visit places they loved to help you feel closer to them. If they loved the ocean, take a walk on the beach. If they loved cooking, spend more time in the kitchen. If they were an avid bird watcher, spend time outdoors.

I unlock my new door and look around at my barely put together apartment. The sectional sofa haphazardly arranged in the center of the living room with Petunia nestled in the corner. The TV on the floor with no stand, unplugged, wires in a twisted tumbleweed. The mountain of boxes begging to be unpacked and put out of their misery.

Gio was an interior designer. He designed and furnished everything from intimate, cozy living rooms to sleek, cool offices, and dazzling, spacious ballrooms. He had such an eye for color, light and pattern. I thought back to our apartment, the one I just moved out of. It was his one true love, besides me.

Original puritan pine, herringbone hardwood floors with crown baseboard molding. Picture rails on cream walls with hand-picked brass sconces. An acid washed fireplace. Green painted cabinets with glass. White quartz countertops. He spent so much time making that place his own.

Gio worked for the contractor who was in charge of renovations to several apartments. Each apartment on this floor had similar features—the picture rails, the pine floors, brass fixtures, built-in shelves.

Our apartment was adorned with dazzling Persian rugs worth more than my college tuition, and carefully selected designer drapes to complement the rugs. An off-kilter gallery wall with bronze accents, a custom oak coat rack, and a media console with a built-in record player.

I never bothered to install the Tiffany-style chandelier Gio insisted on having—and begged me to get while he was in hospice before he died. It was still in the storage unit. I might have lived there longer, but the apartment was still Gio's design.

I sit down on the floor and stare up at the big, big windows that face the street. I have no rug with matching drapes. No coat rack. When I decided to give up the apartment, I put everything Gio had selected in storage. Holding onto everything neither hastened nor eased the grieving process, and while I didn't want to throw everything out, I couldn't bear to look at it.

Even this new apartment, this place, this building, still has Gio in its DNA. I'm comforted by the fact he is still somewhere in my home, even if he is just in the walls.

I hope I can make this place my home now. I have to. Otherwise, I feel like I'll be back where I started. This move has to mean something. It will be the start of my new life. Where I'm not afraid to talk to people. Where I will find happiness, in whatever form it comes in. And if I can't, I will force myself to.

I ask myself the same question I have been asking myself since the day I told the super I could not renew my current lease. I never took chances—until now. I'm embarrassed by it, but anyone who isn't afraid sometimes is a fool.

What do you do when you have to leave the place where the memories are?

I hear my own voice answer out loud. *Make new ones.*

Chapter 2

I wake up this morning with Petunia stretched across my bed farther than I ever thought she could go, and I listen to her soft snores. I lie in bed and imagine my day. Get up. Get dressed. Walk Petunia. Make breakfast. Apply for jobs. Scroll through Instagram until lunch. Apply for some more jobs. Feed Petunia. Walk Petunia. Go to therapy and ruminate on everything that's gone wrong in my life.

I rub my temples, hair strewn over my pillow, my feet twisting in a whirlpool of blankets and sheets. I check my phone for new emails, new notifications, any kind of sign that people still care about me. A reminder for group therapy. A text from an old coworker. An email reminder to pay my WiFi bill. *What's the point of waking up every morning if you cannot find an emotionally fulfilling experience?*

I have done this routine hundreds of times, but something about it this time feels off, and not just because of the new apartment. I feel a weird sense of peace bubble in my belly. This would be my new home, *damn it.* It had to be, so it would be, and I would make it so.

I've had my moments of happiness, of course. I was not always a miserable wench who brought down everyone around her. But for once, I feel a burst of confidence over my situation.

I had been dreading the move terribly. But it was over now, and the relief washes over me in the way a cold shower does, shitty at first, but it gets you to snap out of the panic attack.

Now, I must decide on a new thing to dread.

Work. Money. Food. *Loneliness.*

Do you still get emails if you don't check them? Does the news still happen if you don't read it? Is my life falling apart even when I'm not living it?

I roll myself out of bed, and Petunia follows me to brush my teeth, tousle my hair with dry shampoo, and get dressed.

After I walk Petunia and settle down on my table-designated Rubbermaid bin, I open my laptop to look for a job. Maybe today will be the day I find a new full-time gig.

I have a little nest egg saved up from donations folks made after Gio died, but it's starting to dwindle, and it's going faster than I had hoped. Before Gio died, I was able to pursue freelance painting, picking and choosing my projects because Gio's salary as an architect and freelance designer was enough for both of us.

In the years since he passed, I've worked on odds and ends, finishing up old projects that were long overdue. I do the occasional commission, but they aren't enough to sustain Petunia, let alone myself, in the long term. I need steady work and working part-time at the local Blick Art Supplies isn't cutting it any longer.

I'm applying for pretty much anything I can qualify for—other part-time jobs, illustrator jobs, curator jobs, freelance work. My Bachelor of Fine Arts in painting is feeling extra useless as I apply for jobs at cafes and nursing homes.

I open Craigslist on a whim. I have gotten commissions from there in the past and it's been good for quick cash. An elderly woman looking for a portrait of her family of cats and a couple looking for custom art for their new bed and breakfast come to mind, but weeding through the multilevel marketing schemes, research studies and perverts is tedious.

Then this ad catches my eye:

ARTIST WANTED FOR LARGE MURAL PROJECT

Artist wanted for a large-scale oil paint mural project for a restaurant
located in the West Village.
Restaurant is Asian Fusion cuisine
with down-to-earth, home cooked meals your
Halmeoni would make.
Dragon, nature or tea motifs preferred.
12 ft x 6 ft. Paint will be supplied. $500/day for 4 weeks.
Send portfolio and sketches to j2006@trk.com.

I consider it for a minute. $10,000 for a month's work was more
than triple what I make working part-time at the craft supply shop.
The commission is more than reasonable for the size, but one thing
stands out to me: that large a mural with oil paint, in a restaurant?

It would take me twelve-hour days and a *very, very careful hand*
to finish in that time frame, and it would also depend on how
intricate a design they wanted, and if the surface was suitable for oil
paint. If the restaurant were in operation, oil painting could be a
potential health hazard, as oil paint can stay wet for days. I hope
they'd be willing to close the restaurant at least some of the time,
otherwise it would be nothing short of a stressful experience.

But $10,000 is nothing to sneeze at.

I weigh my options. It would be three months of rent. Or two
months of rent with real food. It's a no brainer. I would reply to the ad.
I can't remember where my sketch book was, so I grab my landlord's
move-in papers and begin sketching some designs on the back.

I'm okay with doing something tea or nature inspired, but I

wanted to be sensitive to the true origins of this restaurant. As someone who can only describe her identity as more American than private healthcare and apple pie, a dragon is something I shouldn't be doing.

Tea. When was the last time I had tea?

This morning.

When was the last time I saw a teapot?

I have an electric kettle, but I also have an inkling they aren't looking for something so modern.

The little red kettle on the chef's jacket.

That man again. That was the last time I saw a kettle.

I lightly draw a kettle with a big billow of steam. I sketch a branch with blooming cherry blossoms through the handle. A finch on the upper branch. *No, maybe a dove. Or an albatross.*

I erase the billow of steam and add a flowing stream of water into a porcelain cup adorned with cherry blossoms and hibiscus flowers. *There.*

I hate it.

I want to do something whimsical but comforting. Somewhere you could imagine yourself going to and drinking a nice cup of tea. Somewhere you could escape to. Where you could go whenever you felt lonely, or strange, or when you wanted to talk to an old friend. I rub my temples. *The very place I want to be in.*

I crumple the paper, and take a fresh sheet, and let my wrist do the work.

Thin pine trees in the background. A large, shimmering lake in the middle ground. A large cherry blossom tree in the foreground, to the left. A grassy clearing to the right, little wildflowers swaying in an imaginary breeze.

A steaming red kettle with matching teacups on a red-checkered picnic blanket. A rattan woven picnic basket filled with treats. Orange frosted scones and berry custard tarts.

A wide-brimmed sun hat. Finches dancing around the cattails in the lake. A man and a woman holding hands on the shore of the lake.

I smile to myself. *It looks like heaven compared to this.*

If this idea is rejected, I might paint it myself. It would make a fine first painting in this new home of mine.

I snap a quick photo and open my email.

TO: j2007@trk.com
FROM: robrien@gmail.com
SUBJECT: Craigslist Mural Ad

Hi there,

I saw your ad looking for an artist to do a mural for a restaurant in the West Village. I am an experienced painter and have six large scale murals (3 in NYC, 1 in NJ, see attached photos).

I live in the West Village and can start immediately. See attached sketch.

Give me a call at 212-001-0009 or email at robrien@gmail.com

Rosemary

I attach photos of my previous murals. One of them is on the side of a building for a recreation center in Brooklyn, one of a Tuscan Villa inside a mom-and-pop Italian restaurant in Queens, one on the roadbed of an outdoor dining structure in New Jersey. I also attach some photos of my paintings—a waterfall in Upstate New York, an elderly couple napping on a bench in Central Park, and a hyper realistic painting of Petunia lying in the sunshine in my old apartment. I click send before I lose the nerve.

I'm not confident I can do an oil painting that large in a month. The drying time of oil paint certainly proves to be a risky factor. I don't think they'll find anyone willing to do an oil painting of that scale, for that price in that time frame. Or they could expect the quality to be less than stellar.

Surely, if they pick me, I can convince them to do acrylic paint in order to stay under budget and in time frame. Now, we wait.

I resign myself to not check my email until after therapy at 2:00, otherwise I'll obsessively check all morning. I place my phone on the countertop, and look for Petunia, who is nestled in her eternal favorite spot—the corner of the couch arm. I cup her squashed face in my hands and give her a fat kiss on her noggin. She barely lifts her head as she lightly snorts in response.

I walk to a stack of Rubbermaid bins and lift the lid off one. Kitchenware. I begin unpacking. I thought I would dread it more, but it becomes therapeutic to find a new home for things.

Spatulas and spoons and ice cream scoops in this drawer, silverware and scissors in that drawer. Pots and pans on the stovetop and in the oven. My cabinet space is limited. I stock my shelves with the odds and ends I didn't throw out: boxes of pasta, bags of rice, instant oatmeal and dry cereal.

I empty bin after bin, but even after an hour of unloading books and towels and trash bags, it still feel like I have a thousand more things to unpack. I sit on the floor, Petunia skittering across the hardwood floor to climb into my lap.

I could be unpacking all day. I didn't know I had this much stuff, as I'd hired movers to haul it all. When you're one person with no one but a dog, you surround yourself with more material objects to fill the void of warmth. Surely a new box of cereal could replace the warmth of a hug.

Is this what makes a house, a home? Unpacking? Belongings on a shelf?

I clench my teeth and bring my hand to my chin, my shoulders hunched. I had relied on Gio to make our last house a home. He had decorated. He was the one always bringing home a new rug for the living room and suggesting a dinner party on a weeknight.

He was always the one full of life, even until all of his life was pulled out from underneath him. When he died, the light was snuffed from our home indefinitely, and I hadn't cared to bring it back. I had stumbled in a never-ending stumble.

For the longest time I thought, what was the point if it wasn't him? If the light wasn't brought by Gio, I didn't want it. I didn't have a reason why. It's just how my grief was. You never knew why; you could never explain. It was as if you'd handed me a calculus book and asked me to teach it to a group of seventh graders. I could read the words and the instructions, but I couldn't explain anything past addition. How do you put something so enormous, so gigantic, into a digestible sentence to a friend who only wants to get a cup of coffee?

In the first year, I insisted if I had left any trace of him, it'd be like his light was still here. The toothbrush in the toothbrush holder. His razor hanging in the shower, scraggly beard hairs and all. His clothes, hanging in the closet, untouched by anyone or anything except dust bunnies. *Architectural Digest* and the *New Yorker* strewn on my coffee table, subscriptions left uncancelled, automatically charging my credit card.

Those things were his light beaming strong and bright from the lighthouse on the rocky island, and I was a little rowboat bobbing further and further from the shore. *In reality, I was the island. He was the boat, bobbing away.* I wouldn't let *anyone* touch *anything*. I wouldn't let my family visit. I wouldn't let his parents take anything.

I kept all of his belongings as a shrine the size of my entire life. Nothing in, nothing out. I had to keep the light on at all costs, and I was willing to shipwreck anyone who got too close.

In the second year, I started therapy. I let people prod from the outside at a distance, never the inside. I kept the lifeline shrine to the bedroom and Gio's old office. I painted, I talked with my parents, and I let go of some of Gio's things.

But no one could brighten my mood for more than an hour or two at a time. I took solace in my grief. We were good friends by this time. I muddled my way through time, feeling like I was waist deep in quicksand. But it was *my* quicksand.

When they raised my rent to $3,500, I realized it wasn't sustainable to carry on like this. At that point, it has been three years. It took all the courage I could possibly muster to admit I had to leave the apartment. It was a disaster and so was my life. I'd been letting grief drive the wheel and I had to be ready to get back in the driver's seat, or risk losing my home.

I had hoped since Gio designed part of the building they'd be willing to cut me some slack and give me a discount on rent, but after the pandemic, things were apparently tight, even for greedy, shitwad landlords.

So I had a choice to make. Move back in with my parents or get a job and a smaller apartment. *I'm ready for change.*

After packing up our old apartment, I realize it wasn't saltines and instant oatmeal in a cupboard and it wasn't unwashed clothes in a Ziploc bag that made a home. It hadn't been unwashed clothes in a closet, or crusty toothbrushes or rusty razors the year before.

The light had to be all on me, and I didn't know what made a house a home in the slightest. I have picked this apart in therapy a thousand times and didn't want to admit that it wasn't material possessions that made a home because I would have to let someone in again after being closed off for so long.

It's people, and the light that comes with them, that make a home. Stories. Good food. Movies and campfires and going for walks around the block. Everything that comes with having friends and family and someone to talk to.

When someone close to you dies, it's not uncommon to lose all sense of yourself. You become a shell of who you once were. A caricature of the worst version of yourself. Sullen and snotty, someone who not even your mother could bear to look at. You don't want to talk to your friends. And to top it off, your friends don't know what to say to you.

"I'm sorry for your loss. Can we help with anything for the funeral?"

"My condolences. Do you want us to bring you dinner?"

"Is there anything I can do? We could make a donation in his honor."

"We're so sorry. You know you can always call us."

Everyone says the same things, no matter who died. You can only hear *condolences* so many times before you want to rip your ears off, Van-Gogh style, and finally get committed. And your friends can only say those things so many times before their answers get shorter and shorter.

"Hey! Sorry we didn't invite you. We weren't sure you'd want to come. Next time?"

"How have you been? We missed you at the book club."

"What's up? I'm good."

"Lol..hru?"

I think back to my last group therapy and the answers everyone gave. We had been talking about ways we are developing our new self-identities.

"I'm learning the guitar, like Jessie always wanted. I'm enjoying it more than I thought I would."

"I started having weekly dinners with his sister. We get McDonalds with the kids. They play in the PlayPlace. It's good for the cousins to bond."

"I actually went on another hike! I had a good time. I surprised myself with how much I liked it."

"I made his favorite food without crying last night. It was delicious."

And what had I said? "I'm moving to a new apartment. I want to find a new job. And I want to love again."

And with that thought complete, my phone is ringing with a call. I hesitate before picking it up, but rush around the counter to answer before it can be sent to voicemail.

"Hello, is this Rosemary? This is Jordan Park from The Red Kettle calling about the mural." The phone crackles.

"Yes, this is her." I clear my throat.

Why does the name Jordan sound so fresh in my head? Why does The Red Kettle sound so familiar? Oh, hell no. Jordan. The Red Kettle. From the hallway. It can't be the same person, right?

"Yeah, so, we got your sketch, and like it a lot so…"

"Oh, I'm glad you got it!" I answer.

I can't believe what I'm hearing. It is definitely the same guy. Before he can say anything else—in a panic—I hang up the phone and turn it off.

I'm an idiot. The money.

Chapter 3

Who calls instead of emailing? I turn my phone on again, hoping not much time has passed, maybe I can blame it on the train or something.

As soon as I can get in, I tap the missed call from the same number and beg the universe to let this man pick the phone up. *The money. The money. I need that money.*

"Hello? Is this Rosemary?"

"Yeah! Hi!" I shout a little too loud. "I'm so sorry, I was on the train, and you know how the signal can be." I hope my excuse lands.

"Yeah, I got you. No worries."

Yes. Landed.

"I'm just calling about the mural. When can you start?" Jordan asks me. He must be at the restaurant. The background noise nearly overpowers his relatively soft voice. He isn't quite as harsh as I remember him.

"Yeah, about that, I can start as soon as you need, but I have some concerns about the paint." I'm ready to explain over the phone how bad an idea using oil paint is.

"Huh? The paint? It's fine. Just come this afternoon, 4:00 p.m." His voice sounds far away, and I hear clanging and bustling on the line.

"Yes, but I really think you should reconsider using oil paint and use acrylics instead," I say to him patiently, willing him to pay attention to this conversation.

"Yeah, yeah, paint is paint." His voice and words agree, but I don't think he's hearing what I'm saying. "My sister got this paint at a huge discount so you can just make it work, right?"

"No. Not all paint is paint," I disagree. "It's going to take a long time with oil. Oil paint stays wet a long time—"

"Just come in, this evening, and we can figure it out, okay? Yeah?"

"Yeah, but I think we should seriously discuss this—"

"Murphy! Quit it!" Jordan is clearly yelling at whatever is going on around him, and next thing I know, the phone call is over.

Group therapy takes place the first and third Tuesday of every month at 2:00 p.m. at Our Lady of Perpetual Help in Brooklyn. As I wait for the train, I unlock my phone and let my thumb hesitantly hover over the App Store.

Curiosity had gotten the better of me in the past, and I had downloaded a wide variety of dating apps, but I immediately felt guilty and cried myself to sleep after deleting them all. My curiosity at knowing who was out there was beginning to pique my interest again after all this time.

After seeing Jordan and Murphy, I realized how much I missed talking and bantering and being around other people. Even though I had been upset, it was the most I had felt like myself in a long time. Being annoyed, being angry, being frustrated were some of the only emotions I had felt—other than sadness and sullenness. Emotions that made you feel more like a human and less like a blobby being filled with antidepressants, Cheerios and ChapStick.

Walking the two blocks from the train station to the church, I shove my phone in my pocket, the dating app undownloaded. I sit down in one of the small rickety, metal folding chairs arranged in a small circle in the damp, musty basement of the church.

Pastor Gilmore stands at the entrance, perpetually frustrated that the group is nonsecular. Other group members file in, with Martina, the group facilitator, closing the door as the last member takes their seat.

This grief group is open to all, but we often have the same members come over and over again, myself included. This will be my second year. Of course, I skip some weeks, but when things are especially bad, I make it a point to show up.

First, we start the opening ritual by going around the circle and saying our names, who we lost and how and how we're doing. I have been here so many times, I think I have everyone's situation memorized.

One.

"I'm Marcus. I lost my wife Jessie in childbirth. I'm having trouble potty training Jenny, but I'm okay. Thanks."

Two.

"I'm Adriana. I lost my wife from a heart attack. I just started a new job, and the new facility daycare is perfect for us. I'm tired, but alive."

Three.

"I'm Melissa. I lost my boyfriend in a car accident. I miss him but I'm enjoying my new relationship. I'm happy."

Four.

"I'm Owen. I lost my husband from a pulmonary embolism. I made his favorite dessert for his niece's birthday party. It was so much fun."

My turn.

"I'm Rosemary. I lost my fiancé to brain cancer. I moved out of our old apartment together. I'm okay considering the situation."

Today's topic is Reinvesting in Your Life! I think I've talked about this topic about a hundred times. We go around the group one by one like in the introduction and talk about how we're reinvesting in our lives without our partners. We are all asked to offer words of encouragement or our own advice to each person after they say their piece.

I'm usually rather quiet at this point in the group session, as I prefer listening to other members. I only offer words of encouragement or congratulations.

When it's my turn to speak about how I'm reinvesting in my life, I know what the obvious thing to say is: "I moved out of our old apartment." But instead, I find different words tumbling out of my mouth: "I downloaded a dating app." Now, I hadn't, but I wanted to—but felt so guilty and couldn't bring myself to. That's the kind of thing I should have said.

The words of encouragement:
"That's so exciting!"
"It'll be so fun for you!"
The words of advice:
"Watch out for scammers!"
"Oh, be careful please, meet in public!"

I nod my head in agreement, silently begging Martina to keep the group moving, but the heckling continues.

"It's fun, once you get used to it," says Melissa, next to me. "It's a little jarring to be looking at other people who aren't your fiancé. I'm sure you'll get used to it though." She gives me a soft and encouraging smile.

My face feels hotter than the sun. I should have talked about the apartment or the job, or quite literally, anything else but the dating app I didn't download. I guess this is it then. I have to do it, or at the next group when they inevitably ask me about it, I won't have anything to say.

I remember when Melissa first announced she was going on a date. Everyone ribbed her for *weeks*. She took it in good spirits, but I'm not sure I can withstand the jokes. Dealing with the guilt is enough on its own.

The group goes through the closing ritual of talking about what we are looking forward to this week.

"I'm looking forward to taking our daughter to the park."

"I'm looking forward to getting my first paycheck."

"I'm looking forward to celebrating our six month anniversary."

"I'm looking forward to starting my cooking class."

What would I say? *I'm looking forward to painting again.* And I say it.

"I'm looking forward to painting again."

I show up to The Red Kettle at 4:00—to find the restaurant not open yet—completely terrified about how this is going to go down when Jordan realizes it's me. I shove any fear down to the bottom of my toes. *I need the money. Money. That's what this is about. Nothing else.*

The Red Kettle is nestled on a West Village corner lot, neighbor to a bustling barber shop. A red decal that matches the one on Jordan's chef's jacket is plastered on the front window. I hold my hand up to my brow to peer in to see a long bench with tables, accompanied by chairs.

The bench backs against a large white wall. Presumably where the mural will go. I hope they will close the place down for me to paint this. There's a bar across the seating area, with a full liquor selection. There looks to be a small sushi bar in the back, but it's hard to tell from the window glare.

I hear boots scraping the ground, and I am suddenly frozen in place, wishing I could teleport to the face of Mars, to the face of my mother, to literally anywhere else. *I'm not ready.*

"Can I help you? We don't open until 5:30."

I scrunch my face and turn on my heel to face him. "I'm here about the mural," I say with as much confidence as one would say, "Yes, I want the electric chair."

At first, Jordan doesn't say anything. Maybe he doesn't recognize me? Or he's planning on how to hide my body. He steps closer, the gears clearly turning in his brain as to where he knows me from. *He definitely recognizes me.*

"Do you know how much that sofa cost?" he asks, his voice considerably more harsh than when we spoke on the phone. *He's pissed.*

"Not more than this mural." *Fuck. Why did I say that?*

Jordan grimaces. "More than I wanted to pay." He fishes for keys out of his jacket pocket and begins to unlock the door.

"Again, I apologize, I did not *want* to step on your furniture. But I had to go." I don't know why I bother explaining this again. I feel a tension headache coming on. This man won't really just let this go. *At least he hasn't mentioned the keys.*

"And the keys! I just needed you to open the door. You didn't even have to give me the keys. Have you never heard of a 'favor'?"

I follow him into the restaurant, uninvited. He sets his bag on a table and begins flipping on the world's longest series of light switches. The small restaurant illuminates quickly, and that definitely is a sushi bar in the back.

35

"Hey, I didn't know you! I still don't know you. Is that really the hill you want to die on? Is this how you treat all prospective employees?" I keep my voice calmer than when I had to explain to my mother that "I am an adult, and I can get a tattoo if I want." I am ready to shout. I want to stamp my feet like a little toddler who isn't allowed candy before bedtime.

"I'm not sure I want to hire you now that I know who you are. I was really in a bind, and you stepped on my furniture with whatever was all over your shoes that cost $250 to clean—stuck me with the bill."

We look each other dead in the eyes. I am an immovable object and he is an unstoppable force. *Fuck him. I'll find money elsewhere. I'll sell photos of my feet if I have to.*

"Fine then, I'll leave. Thanks for your interest." I mock courtesy and try to slam the door on my way out, but it's a soft close door and the bells on the handle tinker lightly.

I whisper all the curse words I know under my breath, and a few paces past the window, I drop my bag on the ground and let out the most feral "*ARUGH*" I can muster.

This is not how I wanted this to go.

I'm ready to turn back and grovel when I hear an "ahem" behind me.

"Rosemary?"

It's him.

"What?" I start digging around my bag for my wallet. I think I have a wadded up $10 bill I can give him as a good-faith deposit to pay him back for the sofa cleaning. *That idiot probably needed to get it cleaned before I stepped on it.*

"Please paint my mural," Jordan says, his voice much more calm than in the restaurant. "You're the only person we can afford. And I really like your sketch and don't want to have to steal it. And okay, fine, I don't blame you for not giving me the keys."

I stare at him. *Are you kidding me? What do I even say to this?*

"Yes. For the $10,000 I'll do it. And we have to use acrylic paint."

He stares at me, the fire back in his eyes, and I see him mentally trying to stomp out the growing flames.

"Why can't we use the oil paint? I've already got it," he asks, seeming genuinely perturbed that I would even suggest such a thing.

"Well, for starters, I don't even know if the colors you have will be suitable for my palette. Second, it's going to take weeks to dry. You can't close the restaurant for that long. That's just me keeping your best interest in mind."

"What do you mean, closing the restaurant? I'm not closing the restaurant." He sounds truly shocked.

"Did you not do any research about murals or the oil painting process? Or any painting process?" I'm in disbelief, but somehow, I knew this was coming. Everyone loves the detail of oil paintings, but doesn't want to either pay the price or take the time for them. You can't have both.

"It's going to smell terrible, and oil paints take weeks to dry." I'm almost laughing at him. *Who's turn is it now, bucko?* "It's along that wall, right? You can't have people sit there while I paint."

"Can you work in off hours?" he asks in earnest. "We don't open until noon for lunch. And we're closed from 3:00 to 5:00 before dinner."

"I can work off hours in acrylics," I say. "There is no way oil paint will be ready to have patrons near it the same day."

Jordan rubs his temple the same way I do when I am stressed and thinking about something. It seems like he's considering my offer.

"I'll have to deduct the cost of new paint from your payment."

There's the kicker. "That's fine." *It's money and I need money. I still get the portfolio piece.* I'm trying to convince myself I can still do this and not k-word myself. It's not really fine, but what choice do I have? *If I can get through Gio's death, I can get through one lousy mural.*

Jordan holds his hand out for me to shake. "You have a deal. I'll give you some cash, half up front. Go get the supplies you need and start tomorrow."

I shake his hand and follow him back into the restaurant as he opens the register. He thumbs through some bills.

"I only have $600 in the register. Will that be enough for supplies? I'll write you a check for the other $4,400," he tells me, handing me a stack of twenties.

"Works for me." I'm baffled by this whole situation. *What made him change his mind?* "Where did you even get all this oil paint?" I gesture to the stacks of cans quite literally in the corner of his shop. "You shouldn't leave this out. It's like liquid gold." I laugh at my own joke.

Those cans go for $80, sometimes more.

"My mother was a painter. I guess I should have known better than to ask for an oil painting here." He laughs grimly.

"She was? Is she no longer?" I ask, wondering if his mother had died. *Of course you wonder if she died, you death-obsessed weirdo.*

"I guess she still is. She was diagnosed with Alzhiemers recently and doesn't paint much anymore. This paint was from her studio that we sold recently," he explains. "She'd want it to go to good use."

"Oh, I'm sorry to hear about her diagnosis. You don't have to explain if you don't feel comfortable sharing." I look at Jordan squarely in the eye for once. He's handsome. His eyes are a deep brown, with his eyebrows bushy and thick, a smattering of freckles across his nose.

For a brief minute, I wonder if he has his mother's eyes. Even while talking about something as depressing as his mother's Alzheimer's diagnosis, his eyes are still bright and cheerful.

"Don't be. She's as happy as she can be and well taken care of with my sister." He gives me a smile, and shoos me away. "Get some paint now, would ya? I want this to start soon. Start tomorrow."

I flatly smile back. "Yes, boss."

I shove the cash in my pocket and on my walk to the subway station, I am determined to make this a new chapter of my life. New job. New me. I unlock my phone and let my thumb hesitantly hover over the App Store before biting the bullet and downloading every dating app I can find.

I wonder if Jordan has a profile on any of these apps. *He probably gets a million matches.* I'm physically startled by the thought of him. *Why am I thinking about him?* I shake my head much in the way one shakes an Etch A Sketch, hoping to clear the image of his attractive, smiling face out of my mind.

For someone who frustrates me to no end, I sure find myself thinking a lot about him on the ride to my Blick to hand in my badge and buy paints as a customer, not an employee. Our first meeting was something out of a rom-com, and I'm hyper aware of my thoughts about him.

Nothing good could come out of liking him. *He is my boss. And he lives in my old apartment that I shared with my dead fiancé.* Surely, downloading dating apps will be a good idea to get myself off this fixation.

I think back to how I met Gio. We both went to the School of Visual Arts; me for painting, Gio for interior design. We were both first-year students enrolled in art history. He sat behind me and would consistently ask me for a pencil, every class.

I thought it was hilarious—what art student, especially one with so much drawing, would forget a pencil? Turns out it was just an excuse to talk to me. I knew I wanted to marry him the moment he kissed me in the stairwell after class the third week of the semester. He was always much braver than I was.

I was a cold February day, a stubbed toe in the dark, but Gio was the warm jacket hugging you tight and the Band-Aid waiting for you in the kitchen. Where I was introverted and quiet, Gio was inviting and charismatic. I adored the large, loud family that came with him, especially the *Tres Leches* cake he handmade for my birthday.

He fit me in ways I didn't know existed. Being in his presence never exhausted me, and he never grew tired of my quirks. He was sweeter than the honey I put in my tea. I was fulfilled before I even knew I was missing anything.

After he died, his family and I remained close at first. But eventually, people move on in ways they don't think they will. Someone gets a new job. They move houses. New nieces and nephews are born. His sister, Valentina, and I still talk sometimes, but nothing like how it used to be.

Gio was buried back near his family home in Rio Grande, Texas. He had moved to New York for school and stayed to be with me. He had always told me his home was where I was, and I wanted to stay in New York. So we stayed, even when he got sick. He only ever wanted to make me happy. And I was so truly happy.

When he died, I felt robbed of my future. All of it was gone. Gio had planned it for me. I was just along for the ride. Now, I would plan it on my own. And I would start with a date.

Chapter 4

It's Tuesday, and after a day of deliberation I am proud to say I downloaded Tinder. I'm prompted to design my own profile and I am stumped. I don't know what kind of photos to use. Or how to write a bio, or literally anything that isn't filling out an explicit questionnaire. I should have asked Melissa for advice. I close the app. I don't want anyone on this train to see me setting up a Tinder profile.

I get off at Prince Street and walk to the Blick—not my own of course. I grab 64-ounce containers of white and black, 32-ounce containers of deep yellow, true red, and cobalt blue. I grab a small container of gold for the heck of it. I hand the cashier a hundred-dollar bill and pocket the rest. It should be plenty to get me started. *I should have brought my pull cart.* I carry the black and white in each hand, the rest go in my backpack. I clamber down the subway steps again, feeling myself getting tired. I nearly miss my stop even though it is only a ten-minute ride.

I enter the building and get in the elevator, and soon enough find myself face to face with apartment 504. It is only after I insert the wrong key that I realize I don't live here anymore. I slump and my backpack falls to the ground, and I hang my head, lightly bumping the door. I let out a ferocious sigh. *Wrong apartment.*

I am bitter. *This should still be my apartment.*

I grab my bag and make my way down the stairs. Greeted by

Petunia, I pass out on the couch.

When I wake, it's 9:00 p.m. and poor Petunia. I take her outside to do her business and begin to prepare her favorite dinner of scrambled eggs. She gobbles them up as if I have never fed her and never will again.

When she is content with her meal, I sit down on the sofa and open my dating profile. *Let's do this.* After my nap, I am feeling desperately lonely and fighting off the guilt of not wanting to be.

I don't know what photos to choose. I don't know what to write about myself. The only thing I know is that I am twenty-five years old and interested in men. I think. *I want to get to the good stuff.* I feel like a preteen giggling at her mother's *Cosmopolitan Magazine. Show me the goods!* I haven't let myself look at other people in three years. And as much as my guilt permits me to admit, I miss it.

I choose the first five photos of myself on my phone. I don't *want* people to match with me. They can match if they want, that's their prerogative. I want to flirt from a distance and ogle hot men.

Once I fill out my profile, it lets me swipe.

Derek, 29. Looking for my partner in crime. (

"Winky face," I say aloud to Petunia. "That's acceptable, right?" I scratch her head while she looks up at me, her big, brown, fish eyes with not one ounce of comprehension.

I read the rest of the bio.

I'm an airline pilot. Looking for my dream girl to go on adventures with. Always down to try a new craft beer.

Okay, an airline pilot. I could work with that. He's not bad looking, either. A bald head with big, blue eyes and pearly white teeth.

I swipe right.

IT'S A MATCH!

Already? I'm not upset by it. I open up the chat function. *What do I say?*

"Hi," I type, taking the plunge.

"What's up," comes "Derek's" almost instant reply.

That was fast. Do guys always reply this fast? Well ...

Just sitting with my dog. You?

Same. Want to meet tonight?

Tonight? Are men usually this forward? It's late. I don't answer while I ponder these questions. Then he messages again.

Let's get drinks and go back to my place

No thanks I don't drink.

Boo. You can still come to my place. Lol

I definitely do not want to go to Derek's place. A painful minute ticks by.

You can sit on my face if you want, my Queen

Nope nope nope!

I X Out of Derek's chat. Maybe I'll try someone else. I swipe left through a handful of men. Is dinner and a movie too much to ask for?

Nathan, 29. Tattoo artist in Brooklyn. Don't use me as your time waster, Lol.

Jacob, 31. High-tech entrepreneur. Crypto billionaire. If I message u, u message back ;)

Reese, 22. Feminist in the streets, mysognist in bed. 420 friendly and def into bi girls.

Max, 27. Fuck this app I'm never here lol. Add me on snapchat maxywaxy448

Ryan, 26. Only swipe right if U can handle this. No makeup on the first date or expect to go swimming!

Am I crazy? Am I using this app right? Where are all the hot guys who pose with their dogs and their baby nieces and post photos of their homemade baked chicken? And then it hits me like a ton of fucking bricks.

I downloaded an app to look at hot guys. You got what you wanted, dumb ass.

What's wrong with me?

Derek messages again.

Fine bitch lmafo you're missing out.

Seconds later...

Dumb whore. Fuck u

Finally...

Only prudes on this app

Why did I even want to look at hot guys? Gio would never treat me this way. I need to think about Gio. I feel my lip quiver. *What have I done?* I lock my phone and toss it across the sofa, startling Petunia. Why would I need to download an app? I'm mourning, right? Mourning girls don't need to look at hot guys or go on dinner dates.

How can I be happy and go on a dinner date when my fiancé is dead? How can I even think about being happy when Gio is dead? I walk towards the bathroom.

I feel trapped in my own skin. I am disgusted by my own actions. I feel so gross, like I need to take a shower to wash the dirty thoughts from my mind. I feel like I have fucked another man and paid him for it. *Another man. I feel so ashamed.*

I strip my clothes and climb into the shower. *Idiot, idiot, idiot. Why did I download that app? Gio would never treat me this way.*

I let the water flow over my skin, mixing with my own tears of regret. I didn't deserve to be happy after Gio died. I don't deserve to be happy when he's dead. I repeat that mantra over and over like I have the last three years.

If he's not here, I'm not happy.

If he's dead, he's not here.

I should have done more.

I shouldn't have let him die.

Even though I knew I could not have done a thing. Death doesn't discriminate. I feel a shiver deep in my bones, and I know deep down, I have to break free of this spiral of thought I have let myself swim in the last three years. My therapy wasn't in vain.

He's not here. Why can't you be happy?

He's dead. He's not coming back.

You couldn't have done anything else.

You're not a doctor. Why weren't you a doctor?

I'm crying with my whole body. I cough up a lump of mucus and spit it into the drain. A tsunami wave washes over me. This guilty grief feels like nothing else. It destroys everything else I feel.

Gio would have never treated me that way.

All guys can't be like that, right? I ask myself the question as if I have the answer. *Gio wasn't like that. I wish I could have Gio back.* I miss him terribly.

But without Gio, I am so, so lonely.

Shampoo. *I don't want to be lonely anymore.*

Rinse. *I don't want to be unhappy anymore*

Conditioner. *I have so much love to give.*

I want to be in good company. I want to be happy. I want to be in love again.

I have so much love to give, and I want to give it to someone, anyone, who will receive it. *How much longer must I wait before I don't feel so terrible about wanting to love again? Why does it feel so terrible? I know I'm ready to love again. Maybe I'm not ready if I feel like this.*

Who decides? I decide.

I don't mind the changing of the seasons, the many sunrises or sunsets I've spent without him. I don't care about the empty bed, or the missing shoes, or the thrown-out razors anymore. I don't even really mind moving from the apartment.

But I am so afraid that if I learn to love someone else, it means Gio will be gone forever, only a memory truly lost to the passing of time. I'll have to find some way to remember him.

I cry the rest of my shower.

I wake up Wednesday morning with a headache and today is the day I start painting the mural. I stare at myself in the mirror and someone different stares back at me. The same shell of myself I've looked at in the mirror for the last three years suddenly looks different. After it hit me last night, how long must I wait before I can love again?

I decide I don't want to wait any longer. I'm ready for good things to happen. I need something good. *Look in the mirror, and they can happen today.*

I am determined to make today a good day.

I get dressed in my painting coveralls that I haven't worn in well over a year. They're a little snug in the shoulders but I will make it work for today. I pet Petunia's snout and pat her head as she awakens from her slumber. She clobbers my feet, excited for the day ahead. Little does she know; it will be filled with much napping and solitude once again.

I go over my schedule in my head.

Feed and walk Petunia. Go to The Red Kettle and apply primer. Start drawing the design. Lunch break. Go home to walk Petunia. Back to The Red Kettle to finish drawing until the restaurant opens. Go home. I wonder how I can squeeze in working on my dating app in there.

Deciding that the issue with my potential suitors is that my bio is not specific enough, I am resigned to coming up with an extremely detailed profile to put off anyone who would think about cryptocurrency as a turn on or take me swimming on the first date.

I know what I want.

A dinner date with the boy next door.

He'd be unforgivably handsome. He'd be sweet to his mother and would bake me a cake on my birthday. He'd call me every night before I go to sleep, even if we saw each other that same day. He would hold my hand when we walk in the park and buy me chai, not coffee. He'd give me a chaste kiss on the doorstep of my building after he walked me home. He'd tell me he loves me while we watch the city roll by from his secret spot, tucked away in a rooftop or park I've never been to.

He'd take care of *me* for once. I'd be his kind of woman and he'd love me for all of me, grief included. He'd say: "Darling, as long as I'm with you, I don't care where we are."

And I'd love him back just as much. I am determined to find him, no matter how guilty I feel. I deserve to be loved again. *Gio would forgive me. He would not want to see me so lonely.*

The dating app is my first step, and if that fails, then I'll try again somehow. I'll ask Melissa from the grief support group.

Feeling confident with my plan, I take Petunia on a short walk around the block after feeding her breakfast. By the time we get back inside, she is content with her exercise and ready for her mid-morning five hour long nap several hours earlier than usual.

I refresh her water bowl and leave out some kibbles for her. It's my first time leaving her for such a long period of time, and I'm worried about her more than myself. I shower her in a flurry of kisses before I grab my bag, paint in hand, lock the door, and make my way downstairs.

As I ride the elevator down the short three floors, I whisper a short prayer, praying I made the right decision. *Please, God, Allah, whoever might hear me, don't let me run into Jordan in the lobby.*

I don't know why I'm so scared of seeing him now, as I'm going to see him in a few short minutes, but it feels like the time between leaving the building and getting to the restaurant is a sacred, untouchable moment where finally all things in my life are right.

The morning air is crisp, even for April. Spring in New York City is my favorite; not even the vibrant leaves of Autumn compare to the baby blooms of magnolia and cherry blossom trees.

It is as if every year the city is reborn along with the crocuses and daffodils. The sure signs of spring are here, littering every block: ice cream trucks grabbing their parking spots after the street sweeper comes by; the fruit cart ladies sitting on their corners, selling mango with chamoy sauce under umbrellas; artists hocking their prints, even at this early hour.

Shops put signs outside, advertising their specials from two for ten-dollar cinnamon buns to five-dollar cocktails. Elegant bouquets adorn outdoor dining tables, and joggers and bikers, decked in the trendiest workout gear in the open streets, make the coming warm weather feel especially imminent.

I smile to myself and snap a photo of a pear tree adorning the side of a brick building to use as a painting reference later. I make my way down the subway steps and lean on the steel beams on the platform. Six minutes until the next train.

I hesitantly open my dating app. No new matches. Of course. I hadn't swiped on anyone since Derek. I open my profile and delete my current bio.

I type out: Reserved woman seeks a funny, college-educated man down for uncomplicated romancing. Pets must be OK.

There. That has to be off-putting enough to scare off the assholes and douches, but not *so* off-putting it won't scare off the good guys. I'm satisfied with that. I switch to the feed of potential suitors.

Troy, 28. Wannabe standup comic. Looking for a girl who can take a joke.

I can take a joke I think to myself and swipe right before I can stop myself. No match. Maybe he hasn't seen me yet.

I lock my phone as the train arrives, ready to focus on art, and only art. I'm here to do a job. Thinking about painting makes my anxiety grow. It has been a long time since I painted something of this scale. I know it's like riding a bike, once you get on and start pedaling, you remember how to do it, and all is well. It is the getting on part that makes me, and everyone else who is afraid to ride a bike, so nervous.

The train arrives at the station quickly, as it's only a stop away. I could easily walk there, but with the paint in my bag, I don't want to arrive looking like I ran a marathon. Sure enough, the restaurant has the lights on, and I can see a figure moving in the back. I try to open the door, but the bells only jingle. It's locked.

I try rapping the glass door gently, waving my hands wildly, anything to get Jordan's attention. I know he's in there. He's wearing a chef's white uniform with an embroidered patch on the breast pocket. He seems to be mopping. It sounds like he has loud music playing from the back. He's completely undisturbed by my knocking and waving.

I still can't get his attention after knocking one more time, so my only choice is to call him and let him know I'm here.

I select the contact, Jordan (Mural), and click "call".

"Hello?"

"It's Rosemary O'Brien. I'm here to paint the mural. I'm out front. Can you let me in? The door is locked."

"Huh?" He answers, looking up. Jordan walks towards the door and pulls it open with ease. "It's unlocked." Jordan laughs, mop still in hand. "You just have to pull on it."

I am immediately, unabashedly embarrassed. *I knew I should have yanked on it harder. God, why does that sound so dirty?* I turn an ungodly shade of tomato red, apologizing profusely.

"Sorry. I didn't want it to look like I was trying to break in … I figured it was best to call you."

"It's fine." Jordan drops his mop in a bucket. "So, I guess I'll show you around you as part of your orientation. The official tour if you will." I follow him as he walks towards the back. The restaurant is L-shaped with the sushi bar at the base of the L.

"The bathroom and my office are that way." He points to a long dark hallway.

"Kitchen is here. Don't come in unless you have non-slip shoes." Jordan points to a set of swinging double doors. "You might recognize my sous chef, Murphy, from the couch incident."

I nod my head in agreement. "Non-slip shoes. Kitchen. Got it."

We retrace our steps towards the front of the restaurant. He points to the long blank wall I suspected yesterday would be the mural canvas. "This is where I want the mural to go. You can use this entire wall. Just don't get paint on the floor or the bench. I already have tarps and a step ladder in the back of the kitchen." My 5'4 height is no match for a twelve-foot ceiling, unfortunately. His grin is infectious, and I *almost* want to smile back at him, as if it weren't seven o'clock in the morning.

"Thanks. I'm going to get started with primer and sketching the design. Should I get the tarps?" I ask him.

"I'll get them. You don't have non-slip shoes." He glances down at my red sneakers. The very same ones I stepped on his couch with. He disappears behind the double doors, *swishing* and *swooshing* behind him.

I grab the primer out of my painting bag, and a large roller. I take my pencil case out and set it on the table in front of me. I size up my canvas.

First, there's crown molding at the top by the ceiling. That takes at least a foot off the canvas. The bench is about three feet up on the wall. Does he want me to paint under the bench? We'd have to remove it. *This is a disaster.* This canvas is really more like six feet by six feet. *This is bad news. How did I not see it before?*

Chapter 5

Jordan returns, a stack of tarps over one shoulder, the step ladder in the other arm. He now has his sleeves rolled up, showing off his tattoos. A set of kitchen knives on the left and a sharp rose on the right. For a moment, I am utterly distracted and unable to deliver my bad news.

Why am I even noticing him?! I kick myself internally. *Focus on the art.*

"So, we have a bit of a problem," I start, trying to work up my confidence. "I don't really have a twelve by six canvas here. Your bench cuts off at the three-foot mark, and your crown molding cuts off at about the eleven-foot mark." I show Jordan my measurements using my tape measure.

"I could paint under the bench, but no one would see it, and you risk it getting scuffed by feet. Additionally, we'd have to remove this whole bench or risk the continuity of the painting. And I don't think you want me painting over the crown molding."

Jordan looks like I just tasered him. He is not my first incompetent client, and I doubt he'll be the last. Luckily, the ball is in my court with this. I push the image of his forearms out of my head. *Scram.*

I remove my sketch from my sketchbook and fold down the first inch, and the bottom three inches. "It'll look more like this if we account for this main area here," I say, waving my hand towards the bulk of the empty wall above the bench.

Jordan looks at the sketch, his brow furrowed.

"Who measured this space for you?" I ask him, trying to parse out information about how the measurements got so misconstrued.

"My younger sister. She's seventeen," Jordan answers. He sets the stack of tarps on the floor and holds the folded sketch up to the wall.

I don't know how this grown ass man thought that this wall had twelve by six paintable space, but okay.

"Well, as I see it, we have two options. Cut off a foot at the top for the molding and remove the bench. Or remove both," I tell Jordan, crossing my arms. I hope that this entire project is not a series of me asking to make changes due to his ill planning.

"What do you recommend?" he asks me, appearing to genuinely want my opinion.

"I recommend doing the smaller mural. I can make it more detailed to make up for the loss of space," I tell him. "I am confident in my ability to still do a nice mural. You don't want people's shoes on it—if you care about it half as much as your couch."

My eyes grow wide and defensive. I didn't mean to be so sarcastic. "I'm sorry…I didn't mean to take a dig at your couch."

Jordan laughs and takes it in stride. "I can take a joke, Rosemary."

I'm instantly reminded of my dating app.

"Let's do what you think is best," he says. "I trust you to make the right decision. You're the artist. Clearly, I don't know what I'm doing." Jordan laughs at his own misfortune. "Don't worry, I won't pay you less. Just let me know when you want to take a break."

That hadn't even crossed my mind before suggesting we cut the size of the painting. *What's wrong with me?* His forearms, that's what's wrong with me.

"I'm thankful for that," I tell him. "I'm going to start now." I take a glance at him once he's back to mopping, facing away from me. *Good god damn, he's even got a nice ass, too. Focus.*

I'm pouring primer in a tray and getting my roller in hand after covering the bench with tarp, and before I know it Jordan turns his music back on so we don't have to work in silence.

We work quietly in tandem. I draw a new, shorter version of the mural in my sketchbook. He mops. Jordan approves the new mural. I wait for the primer to dry. He sets the tables. I take out my pencil case and decide on a pencil.

Eventually, we begin to chat back and forth. It goes on like this for a few hours. Every now and then Jordan disappears into the kitchen for a while. But he always returns with something in hand and a question.

"Where did you go to school?"

"The School of Visual Arts."

"What did you study?"

"Fine studio art."

"How long have you been painting?"

"As long as I can remember."

"Where are you from?"

"Connecticut."

"What's your favorite color?"

"Sage green."

He stocks the bar miniature refrigerators with reused wine bottles filled with cold water, a bowl of lemons, or a bin of ice. I continue drawing, answering his questions quietly, and adding a few of my own.

"Where did you learn to cook?"

"I taught myself."

"Do you own this restaurant?"

"I rent it from the owner."

"What's the best thing on your menu?"

"The Omakase."

"How's your mom doing?"

"She's just fine."

By 10:00 a.m. I've just about finished the outlines of the mountains and cherry blossom tree. I hear him rustling behind me, to the right, to the left, all over the restaurant, and then it's silent again when he disappears into the kitchen. I stand static in front of my wall, not once taking a break because I finally feel like myself again. I smile to myself, pleased with my sketch. *I am at my best when I am creating.* This feels especially evident, standing in front of my drawing.

I haven't seen Jordan in at least forty-five minutes at this point, only the faint sounds of chopping on boards and stirring in pots. I wonder what he is cooking. I wonder when his sous chef will arrive. *Has he no other help?* Surely if he has $10,000 for a mural, he has enough money to hire another employee like a dishwasher or a server or somebody.

Curiosity is beginning to get the better of me. *Where is he?* I'm beginning to miss his presence. Our chatter was familiar and kind. There is no pass-through window in the kitchen, only the short, vertical windows on the swinging kitchen doors. I know he said not to go in the kitchen if I wasn't wearing non-slip shoes, but how slippery could the kitchen be? Would the floors be blocks of ice or puddles of water?

I quietly walk to the swinging kitchen doors, peeking through the little plastic window. I see Jordan standing behind a counter, massive chef knife in hand, slicing some very delicate looking vegetables. I inch as close as I possibly can to the door without budging it, hoping he'll notice me peering through, so I won't have to get his attention. I push my brain to think of a reason to want to get his attention. *A break. He said come get him if I want to take a break.*

However, the doors begin to swing if I breathe out too deeply. I decide. *This Is It. I'll risk it.* I push the door open. And my life flashes before my eyes.

It's like a slow-motion montage straight out of a comedy movie.

Jordan—leaping to save me from falling on my ass the moment he sees me take a step.

Me—falling on my ass anyway.

"Hey! What did I tell you?" Jordan snaps, yet despite the angry look on his face, he offers his hand to pick me up off the ground. "You can't come in here without non-slip shoes." He is scolding a child who can't follow directions. I am the child.

I am immediately sore, but not as fast as I am humiliated for falling because I didn't listen.

"I just wanted to let you know…I didn't think it would be so—"

"So what? Slippery? They're called non-slip shoes for a reason." Jordan grumbles and shakes his hand at me, as if to emphasize that he's still waiting for me to grab it.

"So slippery, yeah." I hang my head and reluctantly grab his hand as he pulls me up with ease and leads me out of the doorway. I feel like a kindergartener being corralled away from a candy store.

"You can't wear flat sole shoes like that in a kitchen. The solution we use to clean the floors makes it slippery." Jordan sounds like a disappointed father whose child stuck his finger in an electrical socket. "Don't come into the kitchen again."

"I was hardly in the kitchen, I just wanted to let you know I was going to take a break." I am defensive.

"You were still in the kitchen. I can't afford a lawsuit." He sounds defensive now.

"What's with you and technicalities? I'm not going to sue you because I landed on my ass because of my mistake." I snap at him. *Why am I picking a fight?*

"I need to be careful about who enters the kitchen. You're not wearing a hairnet or gloves or anything. I can't afford a health code violation. Just take your break and get back to work." Jordan rubs his temples with his ungloved hand. "Please tell me you won't always be this troublesome."

"I'll be as troublesome as I please. I'll get back to work now." My break is totally forgotten. *I know why I'm picking a fight.* I look at him directly in the eyes, my own eyes unwavering, for once. *I want to flirt with him. He's good looking. Oh, fuck. I could flirt with literally anyone else.* But for some reason, it has to be him.

"What happened to your break?" Jordan barks out a cool laugh. "Was that it? Falling down in the kitchen and you're done?"

"Yes, I think that's enough for me." I push a little smile back and pick up my pencil again.

I don't understand. One minute, he's friendly and chatting with me or offering me his hand. The next, he's cold and grumpy and snapping at me over something silly. I decide on a thick pencil and begin drawing thick lines for the mountains. I'll finish drawing by eleven add a layer of white over the pencil drawing, and be finished in time for the opening of the restaurant.

We chatter away like we had this morning.

"What do you do in your free time?" he asks me.

"Mostly paint. What do *you* do in your free time?"

"I like to swim," he answers shortly.

"Where's your family from?"

"My mom is Korean, but my father is Filipino and Canadian. My parents moved to America before I was born."

"Oh, wow."

"When did you move to New York?" Jordan asks me.

"I moved for college."

"I moved here when I was five," he counters.

By the time I finish, Jordan is still shuffling behind the bar, where he begins slicing lemon. My phone dings.

Oh, god, no. It's Derek from Tuesday night.

I turn around faster than I admittedly want to deny my notification, but Jordan's face erupts into a huge grin.

"Hey, I know that notification sound! I didn't know you were into dating apps, Rosemary." He's teasing me. *He doesn't really think I use a dating app.*

"How could you have known? We've known each other for a week." I'm clearly embarrassed, the tips of my ears burning hot, redder than cadmium red. "I'm not really dating…just—" I stumble over my words like I'm playing Twister, trying to land on the right color. "Just looking." *Deny, deny, deny.*

Jordan tries to hide a laugh behind his hand, his coffee-stained teeth peeking through. "You don't have to be embarrassed. Everyone needs to get laid now and then." He's clearly pleased with himself, looking sly as if he's caught a little kid doing something they're not supposed to.

I am exasperated. *This is for dates. Not sex. Or is that what I meant by a date? I don't want a relationship. I'm supposed to be leaving.*

"I want to see your pictures." Jordan comes closer to me, his arm hovering dangerously close to being around my shoulder.

"What? Why?" I'm shocked. What could he want to see my dating app photos for? *Is he interested in me?*

"Please, I need to see them, Rosemary." He's laughing, but it's not a malicious laugh. "I just want to get to know you better. There's no better intro than the one you've put online for the world to see."

"I guess you're right." He does have a point, but I need to find a way out of this. I do not want to show Jordan my photos. Not because I am embarrassed by them, but I just know that as soon as he sees them, he's going to prod for more and more of my personal life. None of which I care to share with him right now. *But he's interested. Maybe I should share.*

Jordan extends his arm, palm up as if to take my hand. Clearly, that's what he intends to do as he *ahems* and wiggles his fingers. I reluctantly take his hand, and he brings me to a sunlit booth in the corner of the restaurant. He grins wider than a schoolyard bully about to give a wedgie.

"Do I have to show you?" I ask him, sitting down in the wishbone chair. I fold my hands down on the wooden table, my phone face down underneath.

"No. But I'd like to see them. It'd make you really cool if you did," Jordan says. "I'll show you mine if you show me yours." The more I think about it, the more I want to see his photos. *And know more about him. He's kind, when he wants to be, and he's funny. And he's interested in me.*

"I don't want to see yours."

"Then I won't show them to you." Jordan rolls his eyes. "Geez."

"But I want something in return. Something to make the ridicule worth it. Two can play at this game." I'm the schoolyard bully now, shaking Jordan down for his lunch money.

"I'm not interested in your offer any more than you're interested in mine." Jordan taps his fingers back at me. "But I'll do it. For you. Name your price."

The more I think about it, the more I couldn't care less about Jordan wanting to see my photos. There's nothing in there that would lead me to have to explain Gio, which is what I ultimately want to avoid, but it's clearly getting under his skin, and I finally want to have something to hold over him.

"Let me have a date here. For free." I smile back at him, for once. "With five-star service."

"That's it? A dinner?" Jordan raises his eyebrows and looks like he wants to burst out laughing any second. He probably thinks I'm crazy. But this is a big step for me. *A date. I could do it.*

"Yes, that's it." I purse my lips together and tap my fingers on the table. "Do we have a deal? My offer expires soon."

"Deal."

I unlock my phone, open Tinder and set it in front of Jordan. He picks it up and begins thumbing through my photos, presumably.

The first is me in my old studio in SoHo, painter's apron on, palette in hand. *Back when I could afford a studio.* The second one is right after I had a haircut. Third, I'm posing for the camera in a yellow sundress. Fourth, I'm holding Petunia in my arms.

"This is your dog?" Jordan asks.

"Petunia. Like the flower."

"Not like Aunt Petunia?" Jordan chuckles at his own reference.

"Not like her at all."

"This is a cute dress," Jordan remarks blankly.

"Okay, that's enough." I hold my hand out for my phone.

"Just a sec. One more second please," Jordan begs me, his mischievous smile returning.

"What are you doing?" His thumbs are clearly not just swiping through photos.

"I'm just helping you."

"Helping me? Don't touch my profile."

He peeks at me from around my phone. "I'm *helping* you. You need it."

"My pictures are fine!" I snap at him. "I didn't give you permission to touch my profile!"

"I'm not touching your photos! You have like...two matches, Rosemary! Your profile clearly needs some help."

"What are you doing? Give me my phone!" The urgency is growing in my mind, but I keep it cool. I reach for my phone, but Jordan's grip remains ironclad.

He swats my slippery hands away. "I updated your location settings from one mile to ten miles."

"Give me my phone. I don't want the free dinner." I'm only half joking. The food on the restaurant's website looked incredible when I googled it last night.

Okay, okay, someone's serious." Jordan relinquishes the phone. "Please, fix your bio next. Fucking Christ."

"What are you talking about?" The seriousness from my voice is gone, now lilted with concern for my bio. I worked so hard on it.

Reserved woman seeks a funny, college-educated man who lives alone, down for uncomplicated romancing. Pets OK. Call me whenever!

Everyone seemed to have some kind of gimmick on this app. I wanted to go for something quirky but upfront. Is this how people did this? I met Gio in college. I didn't have to use a dating app.

"What's that supposed to mean?"

I'm startled by his bluntness. "What? No, you don't." I'm on the offensive and the defensive. "I don't want to get laid." I set the phone on the table.

"Rosemary. It's so obvious. What the fuck is this?" Jordan snatches my phone up immediately. "You can't have this."

Does my profile really read that way? "What?" I ask in earnest. "What's wrong with it?"

"It's not a 1960s personal ad. You don't need to include the times of day you're available to contact." He barks out a laugh and reads my bio aloud. "Are you even from this century? Did you even look at other people's profiles?"

I cringe with embarrassment. I did not look at other people's profiles. *Why did I agree to this? The free food.* He probably thinks I'm a total loser. Which I most definitely am, but don't want Jordan to rub it in my face.

"Must live alone?" Jordan started tapping furiously, presumably at the delete button. "Are you an axe murderer?"

"I don't want someone who lives with his mother."

I rounded the table to sit next to him. I peered over his shoulder. He twiddled his thumbs over the keyboard.

"Pets okay? Is there a world where pets aren't okay? Are you looking for a sublet? You don't need to put information like this." He beams a huge smile at me. "Especially if you just want to hookup."

"I don't want to just hookup, though," I said, defending my word choice. "I want a relationship. After a *date*." I said *date* with much emphasis, hoping to just stop talking with Jordan about sex. *I want a date, right? But the more I look at Jordan the more I want more than a date.*

Jordan cackled again. "You're using Tinder, you know that, right?"

"I want sober sex. Stone cold sober." I retorted. "I thought you had to be drunk to have a hookup." I was the one doing all the mentioning of sex.

"Stone cold sober sex. You're definitely an axe murderer." Jordan looks me in the eye. "You don't have to be drunk to hook up, you freak." He gives me a big, playful smile and I can't help but find myself smiling back.

"That makes me a freak? Boy, do you have something coming." I managed to crack a smile back. "I don't care what a hookup is." I reached for my phone, but Jordan yanked it out of reach by standing up from the bench. "I just don't want any commitment."

"Let's see here." He chuckled under his breath and typed something. "Try this." He handed me my phone back with a smug smile. He'd added the new photos of me painting the mural and in the park and updated my bio to read:

Let me draw you for dinner. Looking for a new muse and casual fun. Likes dogs, furnished apartments, beds with headboards and sushi.

"Is this really better?" I asked.

"See for yourself." I settled back on the bench staring at my new profile. I thumbed through a few profiles. Left, left, left, left. Maybe it would take a while to get a new cohort of men.

"Give that back to me," he said, with his mouth full. "How did you not have *any* matches?"

He swiped left on a few more guys. "What about this one?"

"I don't swipe right on anyone," I answer. It's true. I'm extremely picky.

Jordan's face twists into a messed-up smile. It's obvious I don't swipe on anyone. *I wonder why.*

"What about this guy?" Jordan holds the phone in front of my face.

> Ethan, 26. Will be your personal chef if you hold my hand. My mom thinks I'm handsome.

"He seems...okay." I mull it over. He is kind of handsome. He doen't have anything on Jordan, but he isn't ugly. He has kind eyes. "I don't know though; I don't want to owe him anything if he cooks for me."

"I'll swipe for you, but I won't hold his hand for you, Rosemary." Jordan looks up at me. "Just try one date. You can use your free dinner for this date if you swipe on him." It sounds like a question.

"Fine, swipe on him." I snatch the phone and swipe right.

IT'S A MATCH!

"I'll have my date here."

Jordan seems to regret his offer as soon as I match.

"What?"

"Yes. You will." Jordan bites his lip ever so slightly and pushes his bangs out of his eyes. He shovels more edamame into his mouth. "I have to get ready for the dinner service soon. Are you hanging around here?" he asks.

"I'll go home." I stand up.

Jordan stretches his arms and back, his eyes catching the late winter sunlight streaming through the window. His olive skin glows in the golden light. My eyes linger on his face a second too long and his eyes catch mine again.

He purses his lips and motions toward the door. "Get outta here, you sex fiend. Let me know when your date is." He's clearly teasing me, and the fact is, I probably look to have the sex appeal of a nun.

I scurry towards the door, eager to lose myself in painting at home, and not dating. *Or sex.* I wave goodbye and before Jordan can get another word out, I yank the door open, and burst outside.

Later that night, I have to psych myself up to message Ethan, who still has not messaged me. I look at my rumpled self in the mirror.

My red hair is tangled in the worst way, my green eyes look sullen, and my dark circles are darker than they've ever been. It's the same look I've rocked for the last three years. I decide I'll get my act together tomorrow, just like I've also said the last three years.

You can do this. Come on. Just do it.

Hey there.

Ding. That was fast. Maybe all men really are this fast at texting back.

Hey there, you. How are you doing tonight?

I'm doing well. What are you up to?

Just watching some Netflix. I think you're really pretty btw, that's why I swiped on you...

I blush, even though there's no chance Ethan can see me.

Hehe thank you.

I think you're really cute too.

He is cute. He has mousy brown hair, a crooked nose and a toothy smile. He is handsome in a way that makes you think he'd take you to the school dance and kiss you on your doorstep before meeting your father for the first time. *That's not the way Jordan makes me feel.*

Aww, I'm blushing. Would you want to get coffee sometime?

I'd love to, actually.

Am I really doing this?

But I work really early in the morning. It'd have to be early in the morning or in the afternoon.

I can do it in the morning. How does tomorrow at Sheila's at 7:30 sound?

I think about it. Sheila's isn't too far from The Red Kettle. I could easily make it there by eight.

I'll see you there.

I'm antsy for tomorrow morning as I get ready for bed. I've already taken Petunia on an extra-long walk around the neighborhood park, and she's had enough of my funny business. The more I think about it, the more excited I am. It's just a coffee date. Totally lowkey. I can handle it. *I am ready to get coffee with a handsome stranger.*

After my shower, I take the time to detangle my hair. It's a lengthy process and one I don't do often. I'll wear it long and curly and then tie it up as best I can when it's time to start painting. I don't want to wear the coveralls again, so I lay out a worn T-shirt and overalls.

I crawl into bed with light thoughts in my mind for the first time in a while.

Would he be the man to hold my hand when we walk in the park? Would he talk about baseball with my father and kiss me on the doorstep?

Even though I barely know him, I hope he is. I don't want to date. I just wanted to love.

Chapter 6

It's 7:25 on Thursday morning and I'm standing outside Shelia's dressed in my yellow T-shirt and overalls when I see a man who *could* be Ethan walking up the sidewalk. When he waves me down, I know it's him. I wave back eagerly and smile as prettily as I can manage. "Hey! It's Rosemary, from Tinder."

He looks me up and down, clearly checking out and judging my outfit, and he seems less than impressed. Ethan has yet to say anything, so I jump to explain the paint covered overalls. "I'm a painter. I have a painting right after our little get together." *It's 7:30, he knows I have to go to work, did he really expect me to dress up?*

"Gotcha. Want to get something to drink?" He doesn't even wait for an answer before going inside.

What's with this guy? He seemed really interested in me last night. *He must be disappointed or I'm not what he expected.*

I go in after him, and stand in line close to him, unsure if I should stand beside Ethan or behind him. Is it rude to expect he'd pay for my drink? He orders for himself, not asking if I want anything. *That's fine. I can pay for my own drink.*

I order a lemon tea and walk toward the pickup counter where Ethan is standing.

"So, where do you work?" I attempt to start a conversation.

"I work for a marketing firm." Ethan sounds bored with my question, like a teenager talking back to their mother about missing curfew. "Where do you work again? What's with the paint covered overalls?" He gestures broadly to my outfit. I know I didn't dress to impress exactly, but I wasn't a disaster today.

"I'm a painter. I'm painting a mural a couple of blocks over."

"Oh, yeah, you mentioned that."

Yes, I did mention that dickhead.

The barista calls out "Large Americano for Ethan!" and he grabs the drink and heads to the condiments counter. *Probably to pour an ungodly amount of sugar in.*

I wait for my drink and a second later hear, "Tea for Rosemary!" I grab my drink and next thing I know, *WHAM.* I slam right into Ethan, my tea spilling all down his front.

His reaction is my worst nightmare.

"What the *fuck?*" He gives a low growl, like I'm an enemy dog, barking up the wrong tree.

"I'm so sorry!" I'm grabbing napkins from the dispenser faster than I thought possible. "I swear, I really didn't mean to."

I press napkins into his front, trying to soak up Lemon Lift Black Tea and Ethan is peeling them off just as I put them on, but I can't help myself. *I have to fix this.*

"Please, just stop." Ethan grabs the stack of napkins from my hands and takes two, gigantic steps back. I've caused quite the scene, and even though I'm not looking, I can feel the entire cafe staring at me. *At me. Not Ethan.* "I don't think this is going to work out."

"Wait! Just give me a minute and I can buy you a new shirt or something."

Why am I always making a mess?

"I don't want a new shirt."

He gives me a nasty once over before leaving in a huff. I am still frozen in front of the pickup counter, now without my tea. I'm palming my forehead, cursing myself when out of the corner of my eye, I see someone approaching me.

Jordan. Did he just see that?

When he says nothing and hands me a steaming to-go cup, I know he did. I say nothing, he says nothing, and we walk out of the cafe towards The Red Kettle side by side in silence.

We stand in front of The Red Kettle, face to face, drinking our drinks, when Jordan asks me "What was that?" His voice is hotter than my tea.

"That… That was my first date in three years," I answer, my voice heavier than a cast-iron pan. "I didn't know you went to that cafe."

"How could you have known? We've only known each other for a week," he says, with a soft smile, quoting me from yesterday. "I go to Shelia's every morning before work. I am just not usually so lucky as to have a show to go with it."

I scowl, feeling scorned over my bad interaction with Ethan. "It was the guy you made me swipe on last night."

"I didn't make you swipe on anyone. You did that of your own free will."

"With your encouragement. This is your fault." I am smug again, feeling brighter with Jordan's surprise kindness. I take a long sip of my new tea. "Thank you for the tea. It makes up for the bad date."

"That was hardly a date, Rosemary."

"It was a date for me." I turn away, eager to just paint again, not eager to answer Jordan's prodding questions. *I don't want him to get to know me. Because I want to get to know him.* Jordan just had that kind of inoffensive, charming aura about him. He had brought me a new cup of tea without even asking. He just brought it, not expecting anything in return.

Jordan unlocks the door to The Red Kettle, and we stand in the entryway, opposite one another. We are like two cowboys facing off in a duel. *Who will shoot first?*

I look up at him. Jordan is at least a foot taller. He looks down at me, his eyes fixated on mine. *What's he thinking.* We stare at one another, but it's not uncomfortable. His eyes are questioning and full of genuine interest, and I am drawn to them like iron to a magnet. I couldn't tear my gaze away if I tried.

"You just need more practice." Jordan tells me matter-of-factly.

"Are you offering?" I ask, not serious, my voice almost sarcastic.

Jordan hesitates, grabbing the door handle, and breaks our staring contest. "You know, Rosemary, I will offer. Come back after closing for a practice date with yours truly."

And before I can decline or accept, he goes inside. He, back to the kitchen, and me, to the barely decorated wall in front. When Jordan doesn't reappear like I hope he will, I get to work.

It's 8:00 a.m., and I start with the mountains. I mix a sable black and use an angled brush to create the trunks of trees, the base of thick grasses and the shore of the lake. I fill in with the mildest of blues, greens and yellows to create a gossamer base of a field, lake and mountain scenery. I am lost in my own little world for hours, nothing in my mind but swirls of lapis blue, moss green and dandelion yellow.

I paint as if my life depends on each gentle flick of my wrist. I am walking on a fine wire tightrope, growing more delicate and fragile with each step. A blue so blue it makes you tear up and a green so green you are certain the grass is greener somewhere, anywhere but where you are. A yellow more yellow than the happiest feeling you could conjure. I don't even have time to be depressed over the nuclear disaster that was this morning.

By the time I put down my paint brush, it is almost noon. Unlike yesterday, I haven't seen Jordan all morning. I won't make the same mistake again by stepping foot into the kitchen, so I opt for a good, old-fashioned text message.

> Hey there, it's Rosemary. I'm about to finish up for the day. Do you want to look?

After a heartbeat, Jordan exits the kitchen.

"Hey! Let me take a look." Jordan makes his way over to where I'm standing, hands on his hips, inspecting my work where you can begin to see the mountains and the trees take shape.

"What do you think?"

"Looks like a blob to me."

I grimace. "That's a good thing. Your mountains should be done by the end of the week at the rate I am going." Four hours a day is not much time to get things done, but being paid a hundred and twenty-five dollars an hour is not one of my complaints about this kind of work.

Jordan places a hand on my upper arm, and while he probably doesn't think much of it, *it's probably all I'm going to think about for the next week.* "So, I know we forgot to talk about it yesterday, but do you mind if I pay you at the end of every week?" he asks.

"That's fine with me," I answer. It really is. *Do I have a choice in the matter?*

Drawn to his eyes, I'm suddenly self-conscious about the amount of time I spend staring at this man's face. *For all I know, it's a regular amount of eye contact for people who aren't self-obsessed weirdos.*

"Cool. So, about what I said earlier," Jordan fidgets, his hands wringing at his sides, nervous for once. "You don't have to come after closing tonight. Unless you want to. I don't want you to think you *have* to go on a practice date."

"Oh?" I'm intrigued. Jordan always seems sure about everything he says, no matter how incorrect, from couches to oil paints, so it's suspicious he's backtracking. I don't know why he wants to help me so much.

"I mean, you definitely can if you want to. Anything to help out my favorite employee." He gives me a devilish grin, his face practically entirely a smile. "Don't tell Murphy."

"I have yet to meet Murphy here," I counter. "Can I think about it?"

"Certainly."

Shortly after The Red Kettle's closing at 9:30 p.m., I'm greeted by two sweaty, giggling chefs, and I immediately know I've made a more questionable decision than going out on a coffee date at 7:30 a.m.

"Welcome, welcome, nice to see you again, Rosemary!" greets Murphy. His red hair is slicked back either from sweat or too much hair gel.

He pulls out a chair while Jordan disappears somewhere in the back. I am faced with my half-painted mural. Murphy takes the seat opposite me.

"I've heard so much about you." Murphy pours me a glass of ice water, the table set for two.

"I've heard nothing about you." I'm playing hard to get.

"Well, let's get you up to speed, shall we?" Murphy offers me a sly grin. "Jordan and I met in middle school. Him, total nerd. Me? Total alpha. He'd be nowhere without me."

"You mean, you'd be nowhere without me?" Jordan bursts through the kitchen doors, a very full plate in each hand.

I am suddenly starving. I haven't eaten anything all day.

"I'm the one who gave you a job."

"My father is the one who got you such a good deal on rent for this place." Murphy lets out a groan twice his age as he stands up, and slaps Jordan on the back.

"Have a fun date, man!" he shouts as he grabs a coat from behind the bar and slaps a baseball cap on his head.

"It's not a date," I quickly clarify. "It's a practice date. Jordan was kind enough to help me after witnessing my tragedy this morning."

Jordan looks long and hard at Murphy, agreeing with my sentiment.

"That still sounds like a date, dude. Be careful, Rosemary. Jordo over here, total player." Murphy laughs. Jordan grabs him by the shoulder and pushes him out the door.

"I'll see you tomorrow, Murphy." Jordan closes and locks the door and pulls down the blinds in the front window. He turns around and clasps his hands. "Don't pay him any mind."

"I wasn't planning to." *Is Jordan a player? He's too nice.*

"Really, don't take him seriously," Jordan reiterates. "He's full of shit. I just wanted to do something nice for you. As your boss. And as your neighbor."

"I got it, don't worry." I offer a light smile as a consolation prize.

"The least I could do is feed you under the guise of a practice date, right?" Jordan gestures to the two plates in front of us. "Please, eat."

You don't have to tell me twice. It looks so fucking delicious. "What is it?"

Jordan takes a seat where Murphy had been sitting, unfolds a chopstick from his napkin and uses it to point out each thing on the plate. Everything looks so expensive, more than I would ever pay for dinner. Jordan explains each dish as he takes a bite, and I take one after him.

Sautéed pea shoots: "I get these special from a guy to make sure they are just the right amount of tender and crisp. You sauté them over very high heat with chicken stock to bring out the aromatics."

Handmade steamed vegetable dumplings: "These are vegan actually. And I hand make the wrappers every Sunday night."

Saikyo Miso-Broiled Nigiri: "This is made with a sweeter, milder miso paste and is cooked lightly with a blowtorch. One of my favorite things to make."

Aji nigiri sushi: "This is a very light and buttery fish, one of my favorite cuts of fish by far."

Baek Kimchi: "This is my take on a classic Korean side dish. Safe for white people, basically." Jordan chuckles at his own dig.

"It's amazing. Where did you learn to make all of this stuff?" I ask him, my mouth stuffed with pea shoots.

"My father's cousin owns a sushi shop in Japan. I spent my summers there growing up, working in the shop and watching them cooking. I was a dishwasher. It was always my dream to open a restaurant, ever since I was a kid. Food was usually the only constant in my life."

"Thank you for all this." I gesture to the huge plate in front of me, bites of things still remaining. I couldn't even come close to finishing. "Was this part of the practice date?" I ask, swallowing a burp.

"Well…I guess it was." Jordan looks pensive. "I didn't really have an idea for your practice date. I just…" He trails off, looking down and away from my eyes.

"What?"

"Ever since I saw you in the hallway… Can I be frank with you?" Jordan now looks directly at me.

"What?" I repeat. *Oh fuck. Here we go.*

"I didn't mean to ask you on a practice date. I had dates on my mind because of your silly app." He gestures towards my phone on the table.

Was he thinking about my profile?

"I was just concerned. It was luck that you applied for the mural. But you didn't seem too good when I met you in the hallway for the first time. I was going to try to figure out where your new apartment was." Jordan takes a breath. "And I'm sorry for snapping at you yesterday, but I don't want you to hurt yourself."

Does he seriously think I'm that far gone?

"And it felt weird not getting to know you after seeing I moved into your old place. There, I said my piece." Jordan rubs his temples the same way I do.

"I don't hate you. I am just confused." I am almost comical. *What is happening here? He's worried about me? Is that why he changed his mind about the mural and the acrylic paint?*

"Are you pitying me?" Frustrated, I stand up from the table. "Because if that's the case, I don't want your pity."

"No, I want to be your friend, Rosemary. And I'm concerned you hate me."

"What are you talking about?" I'm startled. I thought he hated *me.* "We're friends."

I like talking to Jordan more than I want to admit. I had a brilliant time listening to him talk about fish and food. I had missed his conversation during the day today, and clearly, he had ruminated on potentially messing it up by asking me on a fake date instead of just asking me to come eat.

"Just don't lie to me about wanting to feed me. It was so good. You don't have to lie to get me in the door. And to be clear, I can afford food," I tell him. I'm the one doing the reassuring for once.

"Please stay to eat after you finish painting then, please? You look like a ghost."

His question sounds like a command. I know I didn't look well, but do I really look that much like a ghost?

"Every day, please."

"I will." I would not say no to free food during this frugal time in my life.

"Thank you. That would make me feel a lot better about you being on your feet for so long."

"It's four hours, Jordan." I'm snickering, and he's in a good mood. "Thank you for your concern and for feeding me. But I've survived this long without knowing you. I think I can manage."

"I know, I know. I can't help it. I've been spending so much time with my mother these days. She's rubbing off on me." Jordan runs his hands through his thick, black hair. "She is always trying to take care of everyone. Even now."

"How is she doing?"

"She's doing fine. It's an adjustment for everyone though." He takes a breath, and his voice turns serious. "I moved into your apartment to have more space for her. She can't live with my sister much longer. They just don't have the room."

My apartment. "Take good care of her. And your mother." I crack a light smile, keeping it together for once. There's a palpable chemistry in the air, it crackles more than oil on a hot pan. I'm laughing, like actually laughing. Jordan is funnier than he lets on and I'm walking right into every joke, but somehow I don't mind. It confirms to me that my magnetic draw to his face isn't just a fluke.

"How many sisters do you have?" I pull my feet up onto my chair, I'm still dressed in my paint-covered overalls and yellow shirt. It's my turn to interrogate Jordan.

"Three. One older, two younger."

"And which does your mother live with?"

"The older one. Izzie."

"I see. When will you move your mom in with you?"

"After I renovate the apartment."

A renovation. I'm glad the apartment was getting new light put into it.

"I bet you're going to knock down the wall between the studio and the den, right? It'd make a nice, large second bedroom."

"How'd you guess?" Jordan laughs his infectious laugh and cracks open a bottle of peach soju and offers me a shot, but I decline.

"I used to live there!" I had wanted to knock down that wall as well, but Gio insisted on keeping it in so we could keep the den as a third bedroom for guests.

We talk about everything we love about the West Village (all the cafes), but hate about SoHo (the teenagers), the movies we've watched recently (*Goodfellas, Sleeping in Seattle*), and what we'll do this weekend (open the restaurant, paint). He shows me photos of his sisters, Izzie, Kelly and Mae, and photos of Izzie's daughter, Amelia. I show him photos of Petunia and my houseplants.

By the time eleven o'clock rolls around, we're sitting next to each other on the bench, eyes droopy and hazy from being awake so long essentially playing twenty questions with each other.

"What Ghibli character would you be?" he asks.

"Totoro. Or Ponyo," I don't hesitate to answer. "How do you take your coffee?"

"Hot as hell and black. Where else have you lived?"

"Only Connecticut. What's your hidden talent?"

"I can juggle." The grin on his face is infectious.

"Like a clown?" I giggle louder than I mean to.

"Just like a clown." Jordan smiles softly at me, not offended in the least.

I rest my head on the table. I am tired, and emotionally fulfilled from my evening with this fine specimen of a man. "I should get going. It's late. Thanks for the food, Jordan." I sincerely say my thank you, genuinely grateful for the home cooked meal.

He holds his hand out to pull me off the bench, which I take gingerly, and walks me to the door, plates still on the table. *I didn't even hesitate to reach for his hand.*

"Get home safe please." Jordan looks at me, something different in his eyes than the last few hours, and under his breath he mutters, "This is the part where, if it was a real date, your date kisses you. Except it's not."

"Excuse me, what was that?" I'm laughing. *There's no way he just said that. He only had one shot, two hours ago.* "What are you trying to say?"

"I'm just saying. If this was a real date. Your real date would kiss you before you leave for the night. Expect that on your next Tinder date." Jordan crosses his thick arms, scowl lines on his face. "I don't want anyone to hurt you."

Is he jealous of a hypothetical date he just made up in his head? Kissing Jordan. Fuck. I would kiss him on the first date, except this isn't a first date.

"Even if you tried, I wouldn't kiss you." I say, determined not to let on that I thought about kissing him.

"What makes you think I'd try?" Jordan looks cross, leaning on the front door of his restaurant.

"You brought it up!" I double over laughing. *Is this even happening right now? What's going on with me?*

"I brought it up because I'm your boss. And we're friends." He holds his hand out for a handshake. "I need you alive after all your crazy dates."

"You got it, chief." I shake back.

I turn to leave, waving my hand wildly like a flag. If I wave my hand faster, I can stop myself from turning around and smashing my face all over his like a horny teen.

"This is the part where, if it was a real date, your date kisses you."

I repeat that line in my head over and over and over again on the way home. *Thank god it wasn't a real date. Or even a practice date, because I'd be so tempted to kiss him.*

What made me want to kiss him so badly? Was it because he was nice to me? I had a habit of falling in casual love with anyone who was nice to me for more than a few minutes. The CVS cashier who handed me my receipt. The man on the subway who pointed out I dropped my scarf. The barista who called out my drink. A bully of a man who looked good in a photo on an app.

No. It's because he's a fucking smoke show, and I haven't been touched by another man in three years, and he was just the first. Sure, our chemistry is off the charts, but I can't let that defer me from my plan. *But also, yes. He is nice to me. Genuinely nice.*

A nice man. A kiss on a doorstep. He treats me right and buys me flowers. I will not let this man get in my way. I have to do whatever it takes to distract myself from thinking about Jordan. He is my boss. And lives in my old apartment.

Even if somehow I could get a man like that to fall in love with me, it wouldn't get very far. It sounds like he wants to stay long term in our apartment building. I could not go back to that apartment.

***

A distraction would surely fix this. I run through my list of usual distractions.

An episode of *New Girl.* I turn it off after a few minutes. *This is the part where, if it was a real date, your date kisses you.*

A game of Tetris. I lose after level 5. *This is the part where, if it was a real date, your date kisses you.*

A pint of ice-cream. I'm not in the mood for a caramel vanilla cone.

This is the part where, if it was a real date, your date kisses you.

I bury my face in Petunia's back, her light snoring completely undisturbed. I can't bring myself to wake her up.

I put *Funeral* by Arcade Fire on the turntable. I don't bother flipping the record over.

I put the kettle on and poured myself a cup of peppermint tea but never take a sip. I let it grow cold on the kitchen counter, the steam billowing off to the heavens.

I check the same five apps—Instagram, Facebook, Twitter, Reddit, Tiktok—one after another. Nothing scratches my mental itch. I am in desperate need of human attention. Logically, I know the answer is to make a post in my support group. Or message another member of my therapy group.

My mind drifts to Jordan looking at my Tinder profile. *He is my friend, right?*

He'd helped me with the profile and gotten me a sorry-your-date-sucked tea and fed me dinner. No one did that if they didn't want to be friends.

I had only ever bought one bottle of liquor. I bought it at the corner store two weeks after Gio died. I had convinced myself that in order to survive the pain of losing Gio I had to become an alcoholic. I had taken half of a shot and coughed my lungs out something fierce.

Ever since then, it's lived in the bottom of a corner cabinet. It's probably buried in the bottom of a moving box filled with cartons of saltines and cans of beans, if I had even kept it.

I need it for what I am about to do. I find it and twist the cap off and put it up to my lips like I'm going to drink straight from the bottle like a sorority girl in the basement of a frat house. Except it's more like a terrified child trying to drink out of an adult sized glass for the first time. But still, I manage to choke down a pathetic sip. *Fuck. That was a mistake.*

I wipe my mouth on the back of my left hand, my right hand hovering over the message app. *Just do it, you coward.* I open Tinder. I swipe through hot but unsuitable guy after hot and unsuitable guy.

I have my kid every other weekend. Looking for that unicorn to join me and my gf. I own 16 guns. Only girls with D cups swipe right. Confederate flag.

And there it is.

Jordan, 27. I'll make you tea and feed you all the sushi you want. Find me either in the kitchen or on the beach.

The profile for Jordan. He smiles at my flat face through the screen, dressed in his *toque blanche*, standing in front of the bar at Red Kettle. I swipe through his photos. A shirtless pic of him standing in crystal blue, knee deep water. I screenshot it. *For later.*

A photo of him slicing some salmon in some other kitchen I don't recognize. A photo of him wearing a moss green beanie and sipping an iced coffee in a car. I consider swiping right on him, briefly. It's not like he still uses this app. I bet he would have shown me his profile yesterday if he did.

I see he has several tattoos across his chest. A smattering of roses and peonies. Two koi fish. A tiger crawling across his shoulder. I wonder if he still looks like that. He is muscular, but clearly doesn't qualify to have a dad bod. He is toned but soft around the edges. He looks like he swims a lot. He has a golden tan.

He has no ripped, washboard abs but he still looks strong enough to lift me and then some. His biceps are round and his shoulders broad, like he cradles and carries girls over the threshold of his door every Saturday night, bride-style, and tosses them into his California king bed after wining and dining them with some caviar and prosecco.

Shit. I should not be thinking about Jordan lifting me. Or then some. I shove down my weird feeling that I want to be that girl carried like a game-winning football over the threshold of a door and tossed into a gigantic bed. *Fuck it.* I swiped right on him.

IT'S A MATCH!

Are you fucking kidding me? Why is he swiping on me? To fuck with me?

Petunia is startled awake by my exasperated sigh and gives me a big, puppy dog yawn. "Me too, girl." I pat her wide, Dorito-shaped head and stand up. *I'm going to kill him.*

Chapter 7

It is nearly midnight and I'm riled up. The plan is simple. Knock on Jordan's door, *my old door,* and ask him what the deal is with the match, force him to unmatch me, and leave. I pull up our match on my phone screen in case he tries to pull one over on me and claim he doesn't know what I'm talking about.

Phone in hand, I rap on his door. "Jordan, it's me, Rosemary!" I call. No answer.

"Jordan!" I knock again, press my ear against the door and hear the faint sounds of music and water running. Is he doing laundry? Cooking? Taking a shower? *Fuck.* I'd lose my courage to come back if he didn't answer now.

"Jordan!" I try again. I knock a little more ferociously this time. "Let's go! Open up! It's urgent!" I hear the water turn off and the music stop and a faint *Huh* and I bang on the door with both fists. "It's Rosemary!"

Jordan opens the door, the top half of his head peering around the corner through his chain lock. Water drips from his forehead.

"What do you—"

"What's the meaning of this?" I interject, shoving my phone in his face. "Explain right now."

"Right now?" he repeats.

"Right now." I confirm.

"You're so dramatic."

He undoes the lock but still holds the door open only enough for his face to peep through. I huff and he steps aside and opens the door for me.

He is shirtless. In fact, he is pantless, too. He's in a stupid, little white towel that looks like he stole it from the pool of a Best Western. It's the tiniest bath towel known to man and he has the body of a giant compared to it.

His skin is pink from a hot shower. Freckles on his shoulders. Chiseled chest muscles adorn him, flat stomach with a smattering of hair that disappears farther than I can bring myself to look.

I feel my cheeks burn a painful shade of pink and I know it's traveling to my ears. He looks even better than in his picture. He could definitely pick me up. He could definitely toss me somewhere. Could he tell I was checking him out? *No way. Am I checking him out?*

I feel like a car whose engine won't start, sputtering and wheezing as I try to force my words out. "What? Why are you answering the door in a towel? Are you a pool boy?"

"I believe you said it was urgent. So I came as soon as I possibly could, your highness." Jordan counters. He walks down the dark hallway as he calls, "Just sit wherever. The doctor will be right with you." He disappears into a doorway. Hopefully to put some clothes on.

I am not about to fuck up my only friendship since Gio died because I can't keep my cool seeing a guy naked. *Not naked. In a towel. The tiniest towel I've ever seen.* I step into the apartment. I have not been in here since it was *my* apartment.

He has completely redone the place in the week since I left it. The dining room is painted a dark calypso green. He has a big, dark brown wooden table with metal fixtures and about a hundred books piled on top. Jackets, scarves and totebags strewn over chairs and a mismatched chair at the head of the table.

His kitchen is a chef's dream, of course. A stainless steel gas range with matching hood. A double oven. A state-of-the-art blender, food processor, coffee maker, toaster oven, you name it, arranged neatly on his countertop.

The green cabinets are gone and replaced with sleek, black cabinets to complement his appliances. I bet the drawers are filled with meticulously sharpened chef knives, unstained silicone spatulas and god knows what else. It's like a Pottery Barn threw up in here.

It is not the same place I left it. But I notice some things are the same. Cream baseboard, crown molding. An acid washed fireplace. Brass sconces. The French doors that lead to the balcony.

It doesn't upset me as much as I thought it would. It's just Jordan-ifyed. I sit down on the brown leather sofa I saw him carrying the first time I met him. He has it placed over a plush blue rug with a glass coffee table in the center. He has a flat-screen TV hung above the mantle on the fireplace. His remotes are organized neatly on the corner of his table.

I pet a needlepoint pillow with a house on it and gaze around my old living room. It is still quite barren with not much adorning the walls. Jordan emerges from my former bedroom, seemingly now his bedroom, fully clothed this time. A black T-shirt and basketball shorts. *Yeah, that's a seven-inch inseam.* I should not be eyeballing the size of his shorts inseam or thinking about him sleeping where I once slept.

His hair is still damp. I can hardly stop myself from daydreaming Jordan in the shower, his perfectly sculpted body being drenched by a rainfall showerhead. I imagine what it would be like to place my two hands on his chest. How soft and warm his skin would be. *I need to snap out of it.* I imagine pushing him against the shower wall and punching him in the face.

I take a hot, heavy breath as Jordan makes his way into the kitchen and starts pulling fresh fruits out of his refrigerator. *How is this man hungry after all of that food?*

"What's the prob, Rosemary?" He peels a banana and tosses it into his floor model blender. "Are you done checking me out?" In go the strawberries, raspberries, a splash of coconut milk and honey.

My confidence to confront him is obliterated in the blender with the fruit.

"I wasn't checking you out." I stand up and cross my arms.

"Then why are you here, if not to check me out?" Jordan starts the blender and I wish it were me inside the pitcher, getting sliced up into a thousand slivers. I did not think this through. It pretty much seems that *is* why I'm here.

"Can't a friend just visit?" I don't think he could hear me. He pulls two glasses out of a cabinet and stops the blender. *I just saw him less than two hours ago.*

"You just saw me. Drink up." He pours me a straw-razz-banana smoothie and hands me a glass. He walks around me and sits on his sofa, feet on the coffee table, remote in hand.

I muster up all the courage I possibly can and swallow the grassy golf ball in my throat. I hug myself tighter across my chest and turn to look at him from the island, setting my smoothie on the counter.

"Why'd you swipe on me on Tinder? I didn't even know you used that app."

Jordan looks at me, as if he might be serious for a second.

"Is it illegal to swipe on girls on apps? Are you the swipe police?"

"No." I huff. "That is not an answer."

"Yes, it is."

I huff bigger. "Why did you swipe on me?" I repeat. I need to know the answer, or I will die in this apartment myself. The need to know if he has a genuine interest in me—in the way I do him—outweighs any embarrassment I might have over confronting him.

"Why wouldn't I swipe on you?" Jordan takes a gulp of smoothie.

"That's what I'm asking you! Why are you swiping on me?" I am growing redder. He's avoiding my question.

"Don't worry about it, darling. Drink your smoothie."

I'm starting to figure out the implication of his avoidance of the question. Even though I desperately want to squash my growing attraction to Jordan, I can't help but wonder what it'd be like if he was attracted to me too. Maybe he should be asking me why I swiped on him.

Jordan sits there quietly. Either he was joking and is realizing it would hurt my feelings to do so or he *is* genuinely interested in me. It *would* hurt my feelings if he did it as a joke. Which clearly he must have if he isn't fessing up after this painfully teenage interaction.

I walk to stand in front of him, my smoothie still condensating on the counter. I give him a masterful, bitchy glare and when he doesn't answer, I take a big sigh.

"Fine. Don't answer. Sorry for bothering you." I cut my losses. I *don't know what I was thinking in the first place.*

"Can you move? You're blocking my view." My courage is totally washed down the drain after he turns on the TV.

"I'll leave." I head for the door. It's hitting me that I'm actually disappointed.

"Wait, Rosemary," Jordan stands up after me. "I swiped on you on purpose."

I stop with my hand on the door handle and turn around to face

Jordan, who is now standing in front of me. I must look extra pitiful because he continues.

"Just after seeing your date at Sheila's," Jordan hesitates. "You looked like you could use some help. You were just so…"

"Pitiful." I offer. "Ridiculous. Depressing. Sterilizing. Men can feel their sperm drying up just talking to me."

"No. You just need some practice." Jordan finishes. "I was thinking. I will take you on a practice date. A real *practice* date." Emphasis on practice. "A practice date. So you're not so stressed out during the real deal," he suggests. "As a friend."

"I guess I am a little rusty." I ponder the option for real. I am comfortable with Jordan. "As a friend." I repeat, studying his face, wondering what went on inside his head.

"As a friend. Who just wants you to get laid. And so you can stop scaring the fuck outta customers in any establishment you walk into. See, it's not such a bad idea." Jordan grins. "Will you drink your smoothie and sit with me now?"

I shake my head with a quiet yes. We walk over and I pick up my glass. The smoothie is very tasty. Tastier than I knew bananas could be. He probably put drugs in there.

Jordan and I sit on opposite ends of the sofa and watch *Storage Wars* in silence until 1:00 a.m. rolls around. I could barely focus the whole time. Thinking about how *freaking close* Jordan was to touching me. He fidgeted the entire time.

"I should probably call it quits for the night." I tell him when I can't take it anymore. I gather my jacket and slip my shoes back on. Jordan walks me to the door.

"Come to The Red Kettle tomorrow at 9:30. After the dinner service again. We'll practice."

I mimic him with a small smile and wave goodnight. Jordan

watches me patter down the hall from his door and is still watching me as I get in the elevator. It isn't until the elevator doors snap shut that I realize I'm fucked. I have a crush.

The next morning I wake up feeling like I have cement blocks tied to my feet. I'm simultaneously dreading and looking forward to seeing Jordan. It's not like he *knows* I have a crush. Only I know. And I'm determined to squash it like a mean little kid does a roly poly bug.

I dress in my classic coveralls—possibly the least appealing thing I own—and tie my hair up in the world's most unkempt ponytail. Before I leave, I put on a swipe of blush, hoping to look less like a Victorian ghost child. *It's go time.*

I start my routine of praying I don't run into Jordan in the lobby, and thankfully I don't.

That man must wake up at the literal ass crack of dawn to avoid me because it's already 7:00 a.m. On the subway ride, I swipe through an assortment of men who, in my mind, lack the heavenly male sex appeal and god-like charm of Jordan. *What's with me?*

I feel like I am fifteen again. It's so sweet I feel rotten. This is the first time since I met Gio that I've let myself indulge in and relish a crush. I knew love was a universally occurring, neurotic symptom of living life, but I am shocked with how much I missed being in love and being infatuated with someone. There is something about looking forward to seeing another person that makes you feel like yourself again. And something about Jordan's cheerful, optimistic outlook makes me look forward to seeing him.

I get off the subway and walk straight past Shelia's, not bothering to see if Jordan is there, and straight to The Red Kettle. I am here to work. Not flirt, not chit chat, and not nurse a dead-end crush on my boss.

It is only 7:20 when I arrive and Jordan is not here yet. I lean against the door, taking in the seasonably warm spring air. I flash back to last night. Being fed his handmade cuisine. Accidentally on-purpose seeing him in a towel. *Who answers the door in a towel if they don't want to make an impression?*

What do I like so much about this specific man? And how could I find it in someone who isn't my boss, living in my old apartment?

I like talking to Jordan. He doesn't look at me with pity like my parents do. He isn't jaded or mourning like the folks in my support group. He treats me like a real human being.

Being in mourning and grieving had been part of my personality for so long, I don't know who I am without it. But when I'm with Jordan, I feel more and more like my old self.

We don't talk about how I'm doing mentally. We don't talk about how I'm healing or how long it's been since my anniversary or if I'll mustered up the courage to go through old photos.

Ever since Gio died, I couldn't tell if people actually liked me or if they felt bad for me. But it isn't like that with Jordan. He likes me for me, or so it seems. And he cares that I maybe don't look my best even when he has only known me for a week. He helped me up, replaced my tea and answered the door in a hurry.

Now, *that's* what I'm looking for in a guy. Not a dickwad who gets mad that I spilled some tea by accident and unmatched me after without even giving me a chance to apologize.

It's 7:35 and Jordan still hasn't arrived. I'm debating on giving him a call. I want to get a jump on painting to get over my jitters about everything that happened last night. Another ten minutes pass, and I'm about to dial his number when I see him walking up the sidewalk.

"Hey!" I shout towards him, my arm raised in a half wave.

"Everything okay?"

He's breathless. "Yeah, yeah. Just an issue with my mom this morning."

"Oh, no, is she okay?" I don't have to fake my concern.

"Yeah, she's okay now. She was upset because she thought my sister was trying to steal her food. I had to go over and help calm her down."

I don't even know what to say. Alzheimers is a bastard. I relay that exact sentiment to Jordan. "Is there anything I can do?"

"No, I don't think so. Thanks for waiting." He rushes to unlock the door. "I might be a little busy this morning, but I can check out what you get done around eleven." Jordan lets me know that he has an important customer coming in today around 2:30 that might want to have The Red Kettle cater his wedding and that I will have to come back tomorrow instead of in the afternoon.

"I'll stay out of your way," I confirm as he hurries to the kitchen.

I lay out my tarps and get to work. Today I will focus on painting the cherry blossom tree. I pinch out globs of red, white and yellow paint for the blossoms. I mix red and yellow into orange into blue into brown. A cherry blossom has the classic meaning of revival, rebirth or coming back to life, and I think, in a way, this mural is the cherry blossom of my life.

It's the first painting I've done since Gio died that I didn't totally hate or scrap in the end. My mind drifts to why I stopped painting in the first place. I had no interest in anything after Gio died. Everything I once adored, suddenly lost all the qualities that made me adore it. The color was sucked out of my life. All I could muster was laying in bed, eating cans of condensed soup and spending money I didn't have.

It was a long time before I could admit that no matter how badly you don't want to live, you have to. Otherwise, what are your options? After much group therapy, I learned that feeling better isn't free. You had to work for it, every single day. You had to bust your ass harder than anyone you know just to want to get out of bed.

I am getting there. I had built up the courage to leave the apartment. I am making my own home. I am making new friends. I am finally fed up with being a wilted flower. I am ready to bloom and come into my own, much like the cherry buds that were forced to blossom by the warm air of spring. I have weathered a thousand winters, and now it is finally my own personal spring.

Part of a great painting is letting all the emotions you have travel through your body, your hand and into the brush and onto canvas. I let all my sorrows, troubles and calamities travel onto the wall through delicate but unbreakable flower petals. Now, anyone who looks at these blossoms would see all the pain and anguish I kept buried in the bottom of my soul in a petite, pink flower and be none the wiser, but I will feel better about getting it out.

When I stopped painting, I kept all my grief buried. I turned it into a fortress around my heart. I forbade myself from doing anything that might bring me any bit of joy. It was my private apocalypse and anyone or anything that dared to break down the barrier would be shot on sight. Now, with each blossom I paint, I surrender every guilty, mourning brick in my wall.

I'm ready. I'm ready. I'm ready.

I missed painting so much.

I am so engulfed in my art I don't realize how much time has passed until Jordan is standing behind me, gently *aheming* to get my attention.

"Hey, sorry, I didn't see you there." I step back and allow him to see what I was working on.

"No need to apologize, Ro."

Is that my nickname now? Did he call me that last night.

"It looks great. Beautiful, really." He gives me a shy smile before stepping forward and taking a closer look. "How do you do that?" "Very carefully." I answer with a coy laugh. "Do you want me to show you?" I pick my paint brush back up and dab a bit of light pink in the shape of a cross next to the last blossom I painted. "Start with the base color. Now add your shadows." I change to a slightly darker pink, painting around the arms of the cross, filling out the petals. "Then add your highlights." I dab my brush in some white paint, mixing it with the dark pink for a bright pink. "Fill it out so the petals are rounded."

Jordan nods while he watches closely.

"Then, use a fine brush to add detail. And you're finished. It's very simple, really."

"I think I'll stick to cooking." He laughs.

"No, really, give it a try." I hand him my thick, full brush, already filled with light pink. "Paint the cross." He paints a fat cross. "Now fill it out with shadows." I take the brush from his hand, our fingertips just barely missing each other.

I dab some dark paint on it. "Just like I did, on the tips of the cross," I instruct. Jordan follows my directions hesitantly. "It's okay. If you mess up, I'll just paint over it." I give him a confident smile. "You can do it."

Jordan paints in the shadows and then the highlights for a shaky cherry blossom.

"See, not bad, right? I'll leave it in and you can say you helped." I give Jordan a warm congratulations and smile.

"Thanks for showing me. It's fun, isn't it? I can see why you do this all day long."

I can see why I do this all day long too. "Just doing my job."

Jordan begins prepping the bar by slicing lemons and fresh rosemary. The herbs smell divine, and I am thoroughly distracted by his presence. I can't help but turn back every now and then from my painting to catch a glimpse of him filling the ice bucket or checking the taps or straightening bottles. *I really am like a pathetic teenager.*

By the time noon rolls around, I am satisfied with how my cherry blossoms are turning out. I will finish tomorrow. There wouldn't be time for me to return after the lunch service because of Jordan's pitch meeting.

"Do you still want me to come by tonight?" I ask before I lose the courage.

"Yes. I have a dating lesson in exchange for the painting lesson." Jordan looks up from the bar, knife in hand and it looks more *sexy chef* than *murder weapon*.

"What makes you the authority on dating?" It's my turn to tease.

"Didn't you hear Murphy say I'm a player? I've dated my fair share of girls. And guys, and folks in between." Jordan defends his honor as someone who can give dating advice. "And I've never spilt a drink on someone before."

"I can't argue with that."

"Come dressed in something nice tonight. We're really doing this." Jordan sets his knife down and it clatters on the counter. "No coveralls. Or overalls. No kind of 'alls."

"What? Why do I have to dress up if it's just practice?" I profile and prod for a reason.

"It's to set the scene, Ro."

Chapter 8

When I arrive later that night, the door to The Red Kettle is unlocked and unwedged, and I let myself in. I sit in the main dining room, waiting for Jordan, who according to his text message is preparing some kind of mystery appetizer.

With the lights dimmed and Japanese city-pop music playing in the background, I'm momentarily glad I've scrunched my curls and put on a nicer outfit. I futz with the bell sleeves on my thrifted dress. I'm hoping I come off more as a sophisticated socialite, and less as a freshman going-to-the-prom.

I desperately wished I had something to do other than stare at my half-finished mural. I pray for a text message, an email to answer or even a god-awful Tinder notification so I can get out of my head how much this looks like a real date.

It feels like a real date when Jordan emerges from the kitchen, perfectly polished. He's carrying a pearlescent plate of what looks like pork barbeque and gyeranjjim, or steamed eggs. He's wearing a set of thick-rimmed glasses I've never seen him wear before. *He looks supernatural.* I want to climb into his arms.

His thick hair is slicked to the side instead of falling in his face, and he wears his chef's whites. When he takes them off, revealing an olive green turtleneck underneath, anything I wanted to say is silenced in my throat.

Even though I saw him far more vulnerable last night, something about seeing him in this context makes my heart flutter just as much.

"Welcome to Dating 101." Jordan sounds like he's rehearsed this about a thousand times. "First. *Always* have your first date at a restaurant. It has the perfect set of circumstances to see whether a guy is worth it."

I stifle a laugh. We're really getting into this right away. I nod without saying a word. He hands me a set of stainless steel chopsticks.

"It's the perfect place for a first date." Jordan continues. "Rule one. Your date should put his phone away. His attention should be on you. If he looks at his phone more than twice, dump him."

"Rule one. Got it," I repeat.

Jordan picks up a piece of barbecued pork with his chopsticks and sets it on the plate in front of me. "Rule two. You get the first pick of everything. You decide where to sit. You decide what you want to eat. Don't let him make choices for you. If he orders for you, dump him."

"Noted."

"Rule three. How he treats the waitstaff and how well he tips is pretty much indicative how he'll take care of you. If he tips less than twenty percent or is a jerk to the waitstaff, dump him."

"Should I be taking notes?"

Jordan smiles as he shovels in a mouthful of barbecue as he tells me, "Go, eat!" muffling the sounds of his chewing by covering his mouth with his hand

"What does it mean if the guy talks with his mouth full on the first date?" I needle him.

"Means dump him." Jordan smiles after swallowing, coming dangerously close to breaking the "no chewing with your mouth full" rule.

"So, what's the practice part of this practice date?" I too shovel a pile of barbecue into my mouth and—oh my—it's so good. Heavenly, even. "This is *delicious*, by the way." I enunciate delicious in a way one would say *screw me*.

"Well…we're just going to act like we're on a date. And so when you do the real thing with a guy we pick tonight, you know what to do. You'll have your date here." Jordan offers me another bite of barbecue and I take it from him eagerly.

"Why are you being so nice to me?" I ask suddenly.

"I care about you. As your employer. And as your friend." Jordan purses his lips together into a soft, heart-melting smile. "We talked about this already, remember? Don't doubt my intentions."

"I would never." I take a bite of buttery gyeranjjim. It's my turn to talk through a full mouth.

"So. Back to the topic at hand. On a real date, you're going to have to make small talk. You're good—but you can do better," Jordan instructs.

"Right. So, if you were my date…" I'm stumped all of the sudden. Usually the conversation with Jordan flows right out of me, but I'm caught off guard by his attitude. "I guess I'd ask how your day was. How was your day?"

"It was excellent. I had a pretty girl show me how to paint, and now I'm here with you." Jordan gives me the most genuine smile I've ever seen. "How was your day?" He pours me a tall glass of ice water. *He thinks I'm pretty.*

"I had a good day, actually. I spent most of it painting. At a restaurant and at home."

"What did you paint at home?"

"I painted the city." I pause for a moment, thinking of the best way to describe the painting I started this afternoon. It's the first painting I've started for pleasure, not for money in a long, long time.

My painting is not just of the city.

"What part of the city?" Jordan asks me, sipping his water.

"Only one that exists inside my head."

"Do you have a photo?"

"I don't," I say to him, shaking my head.

"Describe it to me."

I don't know how to say that the painting is of Jordan.

"It's night-time. The moon is lighting the scene. There's an apartment building."

"And?" Jordan swallows, waiting for me to continue.

"And you are looking into the window of this building, into this specific apartment, and in the ray of moonlight, you can see a man standing in his kitchen, stirring a pot."

"And?" he says again, his voice mighty quiet.

"And that's it. That's the painting."

"I'd like to live inside that painting." *Little does he know it's him inside the painting.*

"Maybe you already are," I answer with a coy smile and sip on my water and take a bite of my dinner. *He'll never know.*

"Would you draw me?"

"Only if you cook for me." Two can bargain.

"I already have." Jordan gestures to my plate.

"Oh…I guess you have." I have a niggling feeling I'm going to get bullied into doing a drawing. "Do you have pencil and paper? Or a pen will do. I didn't bring my supplies."

Jordan stands up and motions for me to follow him. We walk down the long hallway at the back of the restaurant, and towards the end he opens a door to what can only be his office. It's a small, cramped room with no windows and a dim light bulb. There's a desk with about a thousand papers and a cup with a hundred pencils.

"Go ahead, sit." Jordan stands in the doorway while I make my way around the desk that practically takes up the entire room. He leans on the doorframe in a way that makes me want to draw him again even more.

"Stay right there," I instruct him. "Don't move."

I pick a pencil from the cup on a whim. It's adorned with white casing and purple unicorns. *How cute.* I finally take a long, intentional look at Jordan. Drawing is an important part of painting, if not more important than the actual act of painting itself. Drawing is understanding how to break things down into shapes and how to reconnect them again.

Jordan has a heart-shaped face with a straight, slightly snubbed nose. I lightly sketch the lines to his face, adding in thick lines for his eyebrows and upturned, almond shapes for his eyes. I add in his full lips and two lines for his neck. I shade in a shape for his lush, thick hair.

I look back at him to see him smiling. I feel the classic Rosemary blush starting in my neck and I hurriedly draw a generic figure for the rest of his body, leaning on an imagined door frame.

"There." I hand him the sketch. Jordan studies it dutifully.

"Again, amazing. I don't know how you do this."

"I studied for a long time, you know." I did. I have a bachelor's degree and three years of experience after that. "I've been drawing and painting since I was a kid." I lean back in the old office chair. "I don't know how you cook like you do."

"I've had a lot of practice, too." Jordan looks solemn for a moment before he says, "Let's go back to the dining room."

"Who taught you how to cook?" I ask, curious about how he knows how to make such fancy food.

"My appa—my father—taught me. He passed away when I was

a kid," Jordan answered.

"I'm sorry." Of course, I am.

"It's okay. It's been many years now."

Of course, it has.

"I also learned a lot from my mother. And now she doesn't cook much at all anymore." He shakes his head. We walk back down the hall, Jordan folding up the sketch I handed him and tucking it away somewhere I don't see.

I know that shake of the head all too well. It's one I've done many times myself. The one where you feel like there's nothing left to do, so all you can do is shake your head and hope it's over with soon. But I know how to respond to this. I've been in his shoes. Grieving someone who is still alive is often harder than grieving someone who's already gone.

"Do you cook for your mom often?" I say, trying to redirect him into a happy memory.

"I do. My umma still says I make my kimchi the wrong way," Jordan says, giving me a light chuckle in response.

"I'm sure she'll get over it one of these days." I elbow him.

"That is if she can remember who makes it." Jordan laughs at his own joke. "Humor is how I cope."

"I totally understand." I give him a gentle smile as we sit back at our table.

"You do? Have you lost a parent?"

"I haven't, but…" I trail off. I'm not ready to talk about Gio with Jordan. I don't want things to change just yet. Then I think better of it, remembering he's already lost his appa. "I've lost others close to me. But I guess I don't truly understand what it's like to lose a parent."

"It really puts life into perspective when you have to take care of the people who are supposed to take care of you," Jordan tells me, putting a hand up to rub his temple. "Sorry to be a downer on our date."

Our date. "Our practice date," I correct.

"Yes, of course," Jordan quickly agrees. "Let's find you a new guy." Jordan holds out his hand, and I assume it's for my phone. I unlock it and open Tinder. I haven't looked since earlier when I saw that Ethan unmatched and blocked me.

I'm happy to let this be out of my hands. Not just because of my guilt about dating again. I'd been working hard on not feeling guilty, repeating to myself: *I deserve love. I deserve love.*

"You pick him out. You even do the messaging. I'm hands off this time." I hold my hands up in a surrender. "I clearly need help."

Jordan stares intensely at my phone. "Ro, you only talked to this guy for like two sentences before agreeing to meet him. You need to talk to them for like, at least a paragraph. That's three sentences."

"So?" I'm not sure what the problem is.

"He could have been a total creep! You need to vet these guys more." Jordan scolds me like a little kid.

"That's why I'm having you help me!" He just shakes his head at me, as if he's had enough. I see him swipe furiously for a moment or two, before he shows me:

IT'S A MATCH!

Mason, 27, I'm a firefighter... I run into burning buildings to save complete strangers, imagine what I would do for you!

Mason looks like a firefighter, all right. *Let's do it.*

"Message him," I advise Jordan, much to his dismay. He winces. "Are you sure? He's a firefighter." Jordan's hand hesitates over the screen.

"Exactly because he's a firefighter." I'm perturbed by his sudden unwillingness to help me with this.

"Give it to me. I'll message him. Yeesh." I roll my eyes in a circle wider than the Earth. Jordan grimaces and sets the phone on the table. I send Mason a flirty "Heyyyyy" and wait for his response. "The more y's the better, right?"

"Yeah." Jordan answers flatly.

"What's your problem? I thought you wanted me to get laid." I look him in the eye.

"I think you should stop using this app."

"What? Why?"

"There's too many creeps on there. I don't want you meeting up with those kinds of guys."

"So? What do you care who I meet up with?" I'm annoyed. I thought he wanted to help me get this ball rolling. *But at the same time, I'm filled with butterflies. At least he cares enough about me to not want me murdered.*

"I care because you're my employee and I don't want you roofied and stuffed into a duffel bag."

"Well, what do you suggest I do?" I ask Jordan, growing frustrated.

"I'll set you up with a buddy of mine."

Is he serious?

"Murphy?"

"Fuck no. Someone different. Rishi."

"Rishi?" I ask, skeptical of this plan.

"Yeah, he's a great guy. I'll comp your dinner," Jordan offers.

"Fine. Set me up with Rishi."

***

The next time I see Jordan is Sunday evening.

I'm feeling antsy for my group therapy even though it's two days away. I have a lot to report on—my dating app, my unsuccessful date, my budding friendship with Jordan. It's safe to say I am feeling a lot and handling it questionably. I made Petunia tough it out at the dog park after the date with Rishi and she is exhausted on the sofa, unable to perform to my high comfort standards any longer. I let her sleep in peace.

I type out a text to Jordan.

Are you busy?

Depends. Who's asking?

I'm asking. It's Rosemary. Do you not have my number saved?

Of course. That dick. He probably doesn't have my number saved. Should I be texting back slower? Doesn't that matter these days?

I know it's you. I have your number saved.

What do you want?

What do I want? A friend. To not be alone. Someone to talk to. *I'm so lonely.*

Wanna watch a movie?

Where?

My place. I have popcorn. :)

Cringe. *What was that? A smiley face?*

Just come down and knock on the door. 301.

I'll be down in 5. Be decent pls.

I'm ALWAYS decent.

What did he mean by that? Was he expecting me to be indecent? My face is hot. I fan myself with my hands. *Why am I so nervous?* It isn't a date. I speed-walk to my bathroom like a dad on a Sunday morning and splash some cold water on my face as if it would make a damn difference.

I am nervous. The last friend I had over was a casual acquaintance in the old apartment, seven months ago. *No shit, I am nervous. What have I done?* There's a knock and I speed-walk to the door, undo the chain bolt like my life depends on it, and ferociously swing the door open.

"Hello!" I'm out of breath, and I have only walked thirty feet from my bathroom to the door. "Welcome!" I say in my best college tour guide voice.

"Are you good?" Jordan asks, his voice stern and dark. "You're not going to murder-suicide us, are you?"

"No, not this time, but please, come in." I open the door further and gesture to my sparse but homely apartment.

"So this is it, huh?" Jordan steps in, automatically taking his shoes off in front of the door. *A man after my own heart.* "This where you keep the bodies?"

"Only on weekends," I answer. I don't know how to use my words.

"I'm not going to be mad at you for texting me. I wouldn't have answered you if I was," he assures me. Then, without waiting for a response, "How was your date with Rishi? Have you gotten any new matches on your little app?"

Ah. There it is. I'm just the charity side-project because I'm so fucking pathetic. Asking my boss to watch a movie.

"I haven't checked. Let's talk about this later. I asked you here to watch a movie. As a friend. Not my dating coach. You're off the clock." I motion to my sofa, Petunia nestled in her corner. I sit down and pull her into my lap.

Jordan turns the corner of the sofa. "So this is the famous Petunia?" He holds a hand out to her nose, despite her being dead asleep. She does not stir.

"The very one," I answer, stroking her forehead.

"Why did you move to this apartment? My—your old unit is something special. But this place isn't...that bad," he flounders, looking around at my obviously sparse living quarters. "I was just curious."

Not that my current digs aren't good, they just aren't as *spectacular* as my old apartment. Tile floors. White laminate cabinets. The fridge in a strange alcove not attached to the kitchen. Livable, but no interior masterpiece.

"Your old place is just a steal for $5k, that's all. I can't imagine wanting to leave it for, well, this."

My voice catches in my throat. I don't want to have to answer this. He doesn't know. I want to keep it that way. He sits in the opposite corner of the sofa.

"That's the million-dollar question, isn't it?" I say, gritting my teeth, determined to change the subject. "So, movies. Netflix or HBO?"

"HBO. You were there for a long time, right? I don't mean to be nosy, but why move all of a sudden?" Jordan prods more. He looks at me in earnest.

"I had some life changes, okay? It wasn't in the budget."

"It's not like this place is probably that much cheaper. It's still the West Village. How much is the rent?"

"Are you offering to pay my rent?" I glare at Jordan. "No? Then stop being so nosy."

"I *am* essentially paying your rent." Jordan responds, leaning into the corner of the sofa.

"You're paying me for a job. I pay my rent." I tell him, and turn on the TV. "If you're going to grill me over my finances, you can go."

"I was just curious, Rosemary. You don't need to be defensive, and you don't have to answer if you don't want to. I just want to understand you." Jordan turns to face me. "I value my employees. If I'm not paying you enough, you need to tell me."

I stare back. *Of course. I'm an employee.*

"Do you really want to know why I had to move?" I ask him.

"Yes."

"My fiancé got brain cancer and died. He paid most of the rent. His parents gifted me twenty thousand dollars after he died. Then, I lost my job and I didn't keep up with my freelance work. I ran out of money." I looked at my lap and took a huge breath and continued before Jordan could say anything.

"I couldn't bear to leave this building, or the neighborhood, yet, and I'm trying to not take on more credit card debt. I'm working part-time. Your mural is my first freelance job in a year."

I feel the tears coming on. *No, no, no, not here, please. Not in front of Jordan.* I feel the lump in my stomach and the lump in my throat growing to meet each other.

"I moved out the day you met me in the hallway. My fiancé and I lived there together. The date with Ethan was the first date I went on after he died."

I ramble on. "My rent is three thousand dollars. I don't know why I told you that. I don't expect you to pay my rent—or I don't want you to. I just wanted to tell you." I let myself talk for fear of the silence.

"Rosemary—" Jordan starts to say before I cut him off.

"You're not on the clock, it's okay," I tell him. "You don't need to say or do anything. I've literally heard it all." More cartoon sized tears fall down my cheeks. *Great. Officially crying in front of my new boss.*

"Hey, hey," Jordan says softly. His round, dark eyes fixed on me. "Rosemary. Thank you for telling me that." Jordan looks at me reassuringly and holds his hand out. "Can I come closer?"

I nod, and he gives Petunia a pat on the head before scooching closer to me and putting his hand on my knee.

He purses his lips closed before saying, "It's okay to cry."

I'm full-on sniffling now. "I'm crying because…I'm embarrassed…for crying."

Jordan laughs lightly. "Why are you embarrassed? You just told me, like, your biggest secret. I half-expected you to cry tonight regardless."

Jordan gently takes my face in his hands, using a soft thumb to wipe the tears from my eyes. He holds my head like a soccer ball.

"What? Why?" I'm suddenly on the offensive.

"You just look like the type to cry at movies." He smiles at me.

"Only if the dog dies." I give him a weak smile and wipe my nose on my sleeve. "So that's it? No condolences? You're not freaked out by me crying?"

"Do you want them?" Jordan looks at me seriously. "I didn't know the guy."

"No. If you say, "sorry for your loss" I think I'll kick you." I laugh at myself.

Please Don't Die

"Rosemary, there's really no need to be embarrassed or scared that I'm freaked out. You're the only one freaking out right now." He moves his hands from my face and I'm suddenly cold from the lack of warmth. He squeezes my knee before moving to pet Petunia. "It's part of who you are. I can't change that, and I wouldn't want to."

"It just freaks some people out, that's all. They find out I was engaged, but he's dead now, and then they don't know how to act around me." I sniffle again and chuckle at myself. *I don't know how to act around me.*

Jordan leans back into his corner. "If you want to talk about it, I'll listen. I want to know more about you. But I'm not going to pay your rent, no matter how hard you cry."

"I don't know how I'm going to ever walk into your restaurant again. You've seen me cry."

"I have already seen you cry, remember? The day I moved in."

Fuck. He did. Too late to be embarrassed, I guess.

"HBO, right?" I do a gigantic sniffle and hand him the remote. "You pick. Guest's choice." Before I know it, my eyes are growing heavy, Jordan's wrapping a throw blanket around my shoulders and my head is on the couch cushion next to his lap.

108

Chapter 9

The first time I wake up, my head is fully resting in Jordan's lap, although there is a throw pillow between us. I twist my head gently, and his own head rests in his hand, propped up by the arm of the couch, sleeping quietly.

Howl's Moving Castle plays at a low volume in the background. I don't know what time it is. I close my eyes again.

***

The second time I wake up, I am in my own bed, alone. Not knowing how I got there, I panic in an instant. *What happened last night? Where's Petunia? There she is.* Petunia is sleeping soundly on the far, right corner of my bed, nothing seemingly out of order. I check myself quickly. I'm clothed. I'm unharmed. I feel fine. *Where's Jordan?*

I clamber out of bed, blankets falling to the floor as I do, and wander into the kitchen. The television set is turned off, only the light above the stove on. Nothing in the house seems amiss. I notice a note left on my kitchen counter:

Ro,

Brought you to bed around 2:30. Brought Petunia outside. Going home. See you later, J

I ponder the implication of *"brought you to bed."* Did he carry me? I don't remember waking up and walking. I was never a very heavy sleeper…maybe I was more tired than I thought. The last time I had a truly restful night of sleep was well over three years ago. It had to mean something that I hadn't woken up. *I feel safe with him. Is that what it is to have a real friend?*

I sit down at my island counter and hold my head in my hands. *What did I do last night?* I knew I had a big, disastrous cry, but Jordan had comforted me and told me it was okay to cry. That's the first time anyone had told me that in all my years of grieving, not even at group therapy. Everyone was always against crying, no tears allowed. It was always:

"Oh honey, don't cry."

"There's no need for tears."

"You're okay, don't cry."

But I'm not okay. I want to cry. It's so freeing to have permission from someone else who isn't myself, to cry. I didn't know how badly I needed it until I had it. It feels it's like what I've been missing this whole time. Permission to be this bad a mess.

And he said he'd listen to me talk about Gio. "It's part of who you are. I can't change that, and I wouldn't want to." The thing about talking about dead people is, how much talking about a dead person is too much?

What if it's only been six months? A year? Two years? Who decides? No one ever knows the right answer, and so I try to only talk about Gio with other people who have dead people to talk about. I know Jordan lost his appa, but losing a lover is not the same as losing a father.

Talking about my old lover is a surefire way to make sure Jordan

110

never takes an interest in me in the way I want him to. But I'm ready to resign myself to the fact he never will. I want to talk about my past like it isn't a ticking-time bomb, ready to blow up in my face at any moment. And I want Jordan to trust that he can confide in me about his appa, and his mother.

I wake Petunia up to feed her breakfast and take her outside in time for me to leave for The Red Kettle. Despite everything last night, I am looking forward to seeing Jordan again and to painting more of the mural. It is looking like I may finish ahead of schedule. I'm not sure how to drag painting this out for another three weeks when in reality, it might only take me one and a half. *One and a half weeks isn't enough time left with Jordan.*

As seven o'clock nears, I rush to get ready. As I enter the elevator, I begin my daily prayer of: *Please, let me ride this elevator alone.* Sure enough, like every other morning, my prayers are answered as I hit the ground floor with no one else in the car.

But in an instant, my prayers are dashed, as the doors slide open to reveal a disheveled, sweaty Jordan staring at me.

"Oh!" I'm thrust into people-mode "Hello!" I say a little too cheerfully.

"Hey, Rosemary." Jordan steps into the elevator. "Were you on your way to The Kettle?"

"Yeah, I was." I take a step to keep the elevator from closing. "Are you going to be late?" It looks like Jordan has gone for a run or to the gym. *He's wearing the same shorts as the other night.*

"No, no." Jordan waves off any accusation of being late. "Come back up with me. Give me ten minutes to shower and we can walk over together."

I gulp. *I don't know if I can handle being back in that apartment again—for two very different reasons.* "Sure!" My body betrays my brain.

We ride the elevator in silence back up to the fifth floor. I follow Jordan to his apartment and try to ease myself out of the oncoming nervousness. *It's okay he knows about Gio. I can talk about him, and he won't run off.* My chest aches to spill everything I know about this apartment to Jordan. All of these years later, the desire to share Gio's memory hasn't dampened, even as I desperately want to impress a new guy.

As more time passes it feels less and less appropriate to blame my inappropriate behavior on "widow brain"—something they call when all you can think about is your widowness, your loss, your grief. I am capable of having a normal, human brain and I am desperate to channel it right now.

Jordan invites me in, and he tells me to help myself to a stack of muffins on the counter. They look freshly baked and utterly delicious, but I can't bring myself to touch one of them. While Jordan disappears into the hall bathroom, I stand looking out the balcony window. I spent a lot of time on this balcony.

By the time he emerges, looking far fresher than I have ever seen him, I have to bite my tongue to keep from talking about Gio. Despite Jordan's overhaul, I can see my fiancé in every nook and cranny of this place. *Just a little. I can manage just a little.*

"Do you know why all the apartments have French doors instead of sliding doors at the balconies?" I ask Jordan. *Here it comes. Hook, line...*

"I don't. Does it matter?"

"The French doors are more energy efficient. They keep the heat in and the cold out. My fiancé was in the architectural firm that designed this building. Every apartment has them." *Sinker.*

"Oh, interesting choice." Jordan hesitates for a moment, probably pondering how far I'll take this. "So you've really got roots in this apartment, huh?"

"Yeah. We were the original renters." I look at my feet. "But I'm glad you're here, in it now."

Jordan smiles. "I think I'll keep them in the renovation. I like all the light they let in."

"Petunia did too."

It's almost 7:45 now, and as Jordan puts on the sexiest bomber jacket I've ever seen, he insists that I take a muffin for later. *This man is always trying to feed me.* I reluctantly take a cranberry orange and stuff it in my painting bag for an afternoon snack.

We leave the apartment and I press the down button for the elevator. I feel hyper-aware of everything around me. The dull buzz of the hallway lights, the way the elevator creaks as it arrives at our floor, and how Jordan and I both reach to press L for Lobby. In the end, I snatch my hand back and let him press it.

"By the way, your date with Rishi is tonight." Jordan says suddenly.

"What?" I am startled out of my own skin. "When were you going to tell me this?"

"Well, I was going to tell you when I saw you at the restaurant— but I'm seeing you now. So, your date is tonight. Be there at seven."

"Thanks for the notice." I hope he can hear my eyeroll, and not my panicked *oh fuck.* I have to wash my hair. *I have to somehow make my face not look like my face.*

"Your face is beautiful, Rosemary."

Beautiful. So I did say that aloud.

"Thank you." I give Jordan the best death-glare I can muster. *How can I like him and still be annoyed with him?*

My day goes by much faster than I would like. I spend most of the morning finishing painting cherry blossoms, and I am once again lost in my own little world. In a city so big, I still often find myself the loneliest one here, and when you feel like a temporary visitor in your own home, it's enormously comforting to have the home of art to visit.

I wish I had been able to take refuge in art more often than I did when Gio died. It was too hard to take refuge in the early days. I felt like I was constantly at battle with everyone and myself. I was convinced I drank, brawled, publicly insulted audiences and disintegrated mentally and physically every day.

It wasn't until group therapy that it hit me: Grief isn't everything you are. No matter how badly you don't want to live, you have to! You must go on and feel the pain of life! And at least today isn't yesterday and tomorrow won't be today.

It was excruciating getting to this point, but as I look at the beautiful cherry blossoms, I'm glad to be standing before them.

***

If I thought grief is excruciating, well, getting ready for my real date with a real guy, not from an app, *that* is excruciating. I want it to be over and done with. I consider canceling, but don't want to deal with Jordan's ribbing later on. *I'm going to get a ribbing no matter what I do.*

I struggle to pick out an outfit as I really only have a few suitable dresses—one of which I've already worn to my practice date with Jordan. I opt for the rosemary green sundress that Gio picked out for me a few years ago for my namesake. *Surely a dead man wouldn't mind me wearing this dress for someone else.*

After my shower, I make sure to put in an ample amount of curl cream in my hair to make my curls bouncy and lush rather than their usual loose format. I hold my hair up in a ponytail and tie it with a velvet ribbon. I put on the tiniest bit of mascara, hoping it makes my eyes look less tired. *You look like a ghost, Rosemary.*

I pull two curls from my ponytail to frame my face and pucker my lips in the mirror as if to say, *Yes. Someone could kiss me tonight.* I deem myself acceptable and pat Petunia for good luck.

I make my way downstairs, of course saying my prayer for an empty elevator even though I'm certain that Jordan is full-swing into the dinner service at the restaurant. The subway ride to my date is even more excruciating than getting ready for it.

When I enter The Red Kettle, the restaurant bustles around me. I see a young girl, maybe sixteen or seventeen years old at the hostess desk. *Jordan's sister, Mae.* I approach her.

"Hi. I have a table for two under O'Brien." I wring my hands out of her view.

"Oh? You're the painter, right?" Mae checks a name in a black notebook. "Yeah. Follow me."

Mae leads me to a private, intimate corner of the restaurant I haven't sat in yet, and she lets me know that when Rishi arrives, she'll send him my way. *Is it tacky that I got here before him? Should I have waited outside? Does it make a difference?*

It really doesn't make a difference, because in a heartbeat, a tall and handsome man appears in front of me with a gentle smile, his deep brown skin glowing in the dim light of the restaurant. He towers well over the table and is dressed in a navy-blue sweater vest. He looks like a character straight from *Mad Men* but in the hottest way. *Wow, Jordan really outdid himself here.*

"Hi there, I'm Rishi." His voice is deep and melodic. *Swoon.* He takes a seat across from me, his golden topaz eyes meeting my own. "You look absolutely beautiful."

My face is most certainly a deep shade of pink. "Hi there back.

I'm Rosemary." I stutter and fumble over my words like a soccer ball. "It was nice of Jordan to introduce us." I want to hide under my arms, but I keep my hands at my sides.

"It was, wasn't it? I don't know why he wouldn't keep a beautiful girl like you to himself." Rishi gives me a pearly white smile. *Not a coffee stain in sight, Jesus.*

"Ah, thank you." I take a sip of my water, not knowing how to accept the compliment. *I've never received so many compliments in a row.* Rishi somehow manages to flag down Mae, who has been running all over the busy restaurant, serving and clearing dishes.

"Let Jordan know we're here?" he asks her kindly.

Mae nods and disappears behind the kitchen doors.

Jordan is the next person to burst through them, and he makes a beeline for our table.

"Rishi!" Jordan claps Rishi on the shoulder, harder than just friendly. "Take care of my girl, Rosemary, here, will you?"

My girl. I know I'm on a date with Rishi, but my heart flutters for Jordan.

"You know I will, man." Rishi gives Jordan the same toothy grin he just gave me.

"I'll be right back with your apps, guys." Jordan insists on hand delivering us our appetizers himself, not letting Mae touch them.

"So, have you eaten here before?" I ask Rishi. "Jordan's food is always delicious."

"I have. Jordan and I were college roommates." Rishi answers with a sly smile.

"Oh, so I bet you know all of his dirty secrets?" I'm intrigued. *But I don't want to spend my date talking about Jordan. I'm supposed to be distracting myself from him.*

"Yes, I know more about him than I ever wanted to know." Rishi

gives me a nod as he takes a sip of his own water. "But enough of him."
The man must be a mind-reader. "Jordan tells me you're a painter."

"I am. I'm painting the mural over there." I point across the way to my half-finished mural.

"Ah, so that's how you two met."

"Actually, Jordan lives in my old apartment, and that's how we met." I clarify a little too willingly.

"Really? You guys have quite the...meet cute." Rishi hesitates before finishing his sentence just as Jordan arrives back with a plate of sushi themed crostinis.

"What are you guys talking about?"

"You," I answer.

"Nothing," Rishi answers at the same time.

I turn my head away from both of them, embarrassed to have said clearly the wrong thing.

"Oh, yeah? Well, it better be good things." Jordan chuckles awkwardly before setting the plate down and leaving without saying anything else. The awkwardness in the air is so thick, I can feel it sinking into my face as if I've stuck my head in front of a humidifier.

I try to lighten the mood by raising my water glass for an impromptu *Cheers!* But Rishi doesn't quite get the idea right away and takes a bite of toasted salmon crostini first so it looks like I'm raising my glass for nothing. I set it down and take my own crostini.

I try again to make conversation, but my heart is beating faster and faster and not because of anything Rishi did. *What about this can't I do?* I was able to go on a coffee date with dickwad Ethan no problem. What's the difference here? A substantial food item? *I'm grieving. I am in mourning. I'm guilty.*

And at once, I have one thought only that I can focus on: *I need to get out of here.*

My chest is pounding. I feel dizzy out of nowhere and my mouth is drier than it's ever been in my life. *I'm going to die in this restaurant. I need to get out of here.*

I lose my focus on Rishi, not giving a shit about what's going on with him. I feel like I'm about to pass out and I'm about to stand up at the same time, and all I do is chug my glass of water. Out of the corner of my eye, I see Jordan coming our way with two heaping bowls of hand-pulled noodles and I hate what I'm about to do. *I need to get out of here.*

I stand up, heading past Jordan without a word to Rishi other than a brisk, "I'm so sorry, I have to go." I recognize what's happening to me a minute too late. It's a panic attack. I'm pushing past customers and patrons standing at the bar and I burst outside onto the front step, and I don't know where to go. I look left, and right and decide to just book it home.

I need to get out of here. I'm doing the wrong thing. I don't want them to catch me in the subway station. As if I don't live in the same building as Jordan. *Fuck it.* I take off my strappy sandals and break into a light jog, but I am quickly out of breath.

"Rosemary!" I hear my name being called. It's not Rishi. "Rosemary! Rosemary, where are you going?" It's Jordan.

I stop in my tracks and turn around. *He came after me.*

"I—I…" I can't catch my breath. *I'm guilty. I can't go on a date when I'm grieving.*

As soon as Jordan gets close enough to me, he grabs both my hands. "Rosemary, Rosemary, what happened? Did he say something to you? I'll kill him." Jordan is an inquisitor, a bounty hunter looking for a thief.

"No. He didn't say anything." I choke out. *I'm guilty.* "I had to leave." I'm heaving air in and out faster than I was before.

"Rosemary, breathe." Jordan takes in a full breath, and raises my hands up, and down when he blows out.

"I can't, I can't," I tell him. "I can't breathe." I shake my hands out of his and fan myself with them, and look around for my escape route. "I have to go." *I need to get out of here.*

"Rosemary. Look at me, sweetheart."

I look at Jordan.

"In and out."

In and out.

"Again."

Again. In and out.

"Tell me straight. What's going on?"

"I couldn't be there. I had to go."

"Where do you have to go?" Jordan asks me, his voice gravely serious.

"I need to get out of here." I answer, my voice hoarse.

"Get out of where?"

"I don't know. This city. My house. My head." I feel tears coming on, but they never make an appearance.

"Let me call Murphy, and we'll go." Jordan pulls out his phone and begins searching for a contact.

"Go where? What about your restaurant?"

"Murphy can handle it. We're leaving"

Chapter 10

I don't ask where we're going. It's late. We take two different trains and a bus, but we still haven't left the city. My breathing is still stressed and haggard, and I'm barely keeping it together. Jordan keeps his arm around me the entire time, and normally I'd read way too much into it, but now, I barely care to notice.

When we get off the bus, we're somewhere I don't recognize. It's a park by the East River. There's a sweeping view of the city at night. The sun has just finished setting and the streetlamps are beginning to turn on. We're walking down a literal beaten path—all that's left of the asphalt path is rocks and dirt—to the water.

"Why did you bring me here?" I ask, inhaling a huge, shaky breath.

"I like to come here when I feel like I don't have a place in this city. Perspective," Jordan

answers. We reach the fence and gaze out at the never-ending bustle of Manhattan.

"Perspective?"

"Perspective."

I turn to face Jordan for an explanation. *We're so far from home, even though we're still in the city.*

"You need a little perspective, Rosemary."

Jordan puts his arm around me the way we were on the train. I notice it more this time, and the heavy weight of his muscley arm acts like a weighted blanket.

"You see how big this place is?" He cranes his head around, looking at the city all around us. "You have your place in it," he says, looking back at me.

I nod, my voice disappearing from my body. *This view is amazing. This city is massive.* It's hard to imagine how many people live in New York when you spend your life confined to a neighborhood, a block, a house, a head. This definitely puts it into perspective.

"Your place is somewhere here," Jordan says confidently.

"How can you be so sure?" I look at my feet instead of the city.

"Your painting. You can't paint like that and not belong here."

Jordan's arm tightens around me, but I am not afraid.

"Look at me."

I look at him, and my eyes have to adjust to seeing him so near. I feel dangerously close to crying. *I don't know where I belong. I hope I belong here. I want to belong here, so badly, so desperately.*

"Tell me where you want to belong, and I'll take you."

Jordan's face tells me everything I want to hear. *You belong here. You belong here.*

"I want to belong here," I say in a whisper, my voice carried away by the wind.

"You already do."

"What if I don't?" I say fearfully. *What if I'm mistaken? I have nowhere else to go.*

"Then we'll go where you do."

"What if this is all I am?" Grief and panic attacks and feelings of dread.

"This isn't everything you are."

Jordan and I watch the city for an hour, sitting on the grass, not touching. I can't believe he put his arm around me, and now that my panic attack has dispersed, all I want is his arm around me again. I briefly consider faking another panic attack to get what I want.

Jordan's words echo in my head—*"we'll go"*? I look over to him. His knees are bent, head in his hands, intently watching the skyline in front of him.

"Jordan?"

"Yeah?"

"Thank you." I force my face into a soft smile. "I'm glad you brought me here. It really does put things into perspective."

"Of course."

"I will find my place. And I'm determined for it to be here."

"I know it is, Rosemary."

He returns my soft smile and stands up. He shakes the grass off of his pants and holds his hand out for me to grab. It reminds me of when I fell in the kitchen. *He's always taking care of me, already.*

"Thank you for being a good friend," I tell him, grabbing his hand, and shaking the grass off my dress. "Let's go home."

As we walk back to the bus stop, I ask, "How did you find this park?"

"I grew up here." He points to a massive entanglement of Y-shaped apartment buildings. "The Queensbridge Houses. The largest New York City housing development. I grew up coming to this park."

"I see. I don't really know what to say other than it must have been rough."

"My parents immigrated here in the eighties. We moved in and out of different homes for as long as I could remember. And then my appa had an accident at work when I was twelve years old, and we moved here. My mom would have stayed here, but she can't live on her own any longer."

I listen to Jordan.

"The only constant throughout my life was food. I was always kind of a punk kid, but my umma would *always* cook for us. No matter what, we had to be home for dinner. And eventually, she taught me how to cook Korean dishes, and Filipino dishes my appa taught her."

"So that's how you ended up with a restaurant?"

"Yeah, that's kinda how I ended up with a restaurant." Jordan gives me a sweet, strawberry smile.

"You are an excellent chef. Your food is always delicious," I say wholeheartedly. "I feel kind of bad I ran out when you just brought us noodles." I laugh at my own misfortune.

"Don't apologize to me!" Jordan snickers. "Apologize to Rishi for running out on your date."

"Oh fuck." I almost forgot about Rishi. "Do you think he'll be mad?

"I'm sure if you explain, he'll understand."

***

Later that night, long after Jordan and I said our friendly goodbyes in the elevator, I build up the nerve to apologize to Rishi. *He really was nice. I was just an idiot.* The thing about panic attacks is that they exhaust you—and make you worried for when the next one will happen. I am absolutely drained when I roll over in my bed, Petunia at my feet, and open up my phone to type a message to him.

Hey. I got your number from Jordan. I'm so sorry about earlier. I don't know what came over me.

Hey. I was wondering what happened to you. I'm glad you're ok. I took home your noodles BTW.

Totally fine. I hope I didn't mess up too badly.

Do I dare ask?

Are you up for a do-over? I promise not to run out on you this time.

I'll think about it...

Fuck.

Yes :)

Yes.

The Red Kettle? Friday night?

Perfect.

I have plenty of time to prepare. I've got the panic attack part out of the way, and I'm determined to be ready after the disaster date. I just need to rip off the Band-Aid and get it over with. I will force myself to bring it up and talk it over at group therapy tomorrow. I will ask Melissa for her advice. I need all the resources I can get.

***

The next morning, my usual prayer is gone from my lips. In fact, I hope I run into Jordan. I want to tell him Rishi is giving me another chance. I want to tell him about how I slept last night; about how cute Petunia looked this morning and that I made my own straw-razz-banana smoothie. I find him waiting in the lobby.

"What took you so long?" he asks me as we walk out of the building together.

"I didn't know I was meeting you."

"Just assume you're meeting me. We're going to the same place. It'd be a little ridiculous to not go together."

"You're a little ridiculous." I throw my head back and laugh like I'm Barbie in her dream car and Ken just told her the funniest fucking joke. *What's with me when I'm around him?*

The train is packed, and Jordan offers me the only seat we can find. I sit, looking up at him as he hangs onto the metal bar above my head. Just looking at him puts nuclear fallout in my stomach. Jordan is becoming the boy I've wished for myself. He walked me home. He comforted me in a time of need. He hasn't baked me a cake, but noodles are a good second option. *He's my boss. I can't have him.*

Says who?

I look up at him. I don't know how to confess. I don't know how I could ever confess to him. He hired me and has been so kind to me, but only in the way a friend is. I would not confess. I would go on another date with Rishi and spend my time trying to take my mind off Jordan instead. *Isn't that lying?*

In the restaurant, I paint. Jordan prepares the lunch service. It's like the day I started. We work in a comfortable, easy silence until I say, "Rishi and I are coming back for dinner on Friday. Don't worry, we'll pay this time."

It's like someone yanked a record off the player. "What?" Jordan's voice is ragged, like someone threw a softball at his throat.

"Rishi and I are coming back tonight. He's giving me another shot."

"What?"

"I just told you. Rishi and I are coming back." I knit my eyebrows together. "Are you good?"

"No, I heard you. Just surprised, that's all." Jordan looks back to his table settings.

It's my turn to say, "What?" I don't know what he means. Rishi was really nice over the phone. "Surprised that Rishi is giving me a second chance?"

"No. Surprised you're going out with him again."

"What's that supposed to mean?" *This is the Jordan I first met.*

"Nothing." He huffs and I feel a forcefield around him popping up, pushing me out.

"What's with you?" I ask, setting my paint brush down. *We were doing so well, now this?*

"I just didn't think you'd be ready to go on another date so soon."

"Well, I'm not, but I have to rip the Band-Aid off, don't you think?" I'm almost hysterical. "I thought you wanted me to stop scaring off your customers!"

"Rishi's not the type of guy to have sex on the first date."

"And you think I am?" *Of course.*

"No." Jordan hits me with the one-word answer and folds his napkins as if he's chatting with the DMV receptionist.

"Why are you being such a…" I stumble and fall a little over my words. *Come on, brain.* "Such a little… Why are you being so aggravating?"

"I'm not aggravating. You're aggravating." Jordan looks up at me. He's got the widest, cheekiest smile. *That prick. He knows he's being aggravating.*

"Please. Let me come here in peace and give Rishi the nice date he deserves. You set me up with him in the first place," I remind him, picking my brush back up to start painting the grassy foreground. I *humph* and wave my other hand at him. "You're just jealous." I want him to be jealous. What better way than to go out with his college roommate?

When he doesn't answer, I know I've hit a sore spot. Is he really jealous? Then why'd he set me up with Rishi in the first place? I'm curious to know now, and I feel like I've got the upper hand in all of this. I look back, and I see the swinging kitchen doors.

***

I sit down in my metal chair. Today's topic: Setting Goals. What goals have we reached?

What's one goal for next week?

Marcus goes first. "Jenny used the potty on her own the first time. I was really proud of her. But she had an accident later that day. My goal for next week is to have her do it on her own again."

Adriana goes second. "I was the top earner for my company last week. But I want to be number one."

Then Owen. "I met my husband's family for the first time since the funeral. I let them take some of his clothes and books. I'm thinking about letting them take part of his ashes."

Marcus puts a hand on Owen's knee. "We all know how hard letting things go is and how brave you have to be for that."

Melissa goes next. "I'm engaged!"

I feel like I got kicked in the chest. *I was engaged once too. Melissa has never been engaged.* I feel like I want to panic, but I force the feeling away. *Melissa is allowed to be happy.*

Rounds of cheers and claps erupt from the group as Melissa shows off her new jewels.

"I think this is going to be my last meeting, everyone," she also announces solemnly, her voice tinged with regret. "Keep in touch, okay?" She looks around the group. We nod as a promise.

"Rosemary?" Martina looks at me expectantly. *My turn.*

"I went on a date. Two actually. I ran out of one and spilled my drink on the other. I have another date tonight

"That's great! We're so proud of you. You should be proud of yourself," the others chorus.

It's not the response I expected. They didn't heckle me. I'm not a court jester. I'm not the laughingstock of America's daytime television. *Why did I think they'd be mean to me? Why was I so nervous?* It's how I treat myself.

"I'm trying to be kinder to myself."

"I think that's an excellent goal, Rosemary." Martina looks at me reassuringly.

On the way out of the group, I stop Melissa to congratulate her.

"Melissa!" I wave her down. She stops in the doorway. "I just wanted to say congratulations." *And...* "And ask for your advice on something."

She looks at me once over. We've never really talked much outside of the therapy group.

"What's up, Rosemary?"

"How did you deal with the guilt?" I gesture to her new, sparkly ring.

She looks at me for a moment, and her face turns.

"How did you move on?" I ask, eager to know the answer. *If there is an answer.*

"I didn't, Rosemary." Melissa answers, a sobering look on her face. "I didn't move on. I just moved forward." Melissa looks upset with me. "Why would you think I moved on? Because I'm engaged now?"

Yeah, that's exactly what I thought.

"I carry Michael and my grief with me everywhere," she continues. "But I know in my heart that I deserve to be happy. And I won't let it take over my life. You should be the same. Don't be selfish to think that all you deserve is grief. Have a good night, Rosemary."

I carry what Melissa said to me as I leave the church and get on the train. "Don't be so selfish to think all you deserve is grief." I know Gio would want me to be happy, even though we didn't explicitly talk about it. I don't know what I'm waiting for.

A direction, a sign, an instruction saying it's okay.

Something else Melissa said stuck with me. "Move forward, not on."

For the last three years, I've felt like I was moving laterally. Everything I did, I was still in copious amounts of turmoil and grief. Everything I did was doused in grief and sadness. *How about I just move parallel?*

In the same way you love both your mother and your father. The way you love both the beach and the mountains, both the flowers of spring and the first leaves of fall. My love for Gio is insatiable. And it always will be.

Now, I just have to move with it, and make room for a little more.

Chapter 11

Later that night, when my eyes are heavier than a marble slab, and the city is finally beginning to settle down, I hear my phone buzzing on my nightstand. *It's him.*

"Hey, Ro." comes the crackling radio-ready voice from the other end.

"Hey." I whisper, the weight my eyes feel not registering in my voice.

"What are you up to?"

"It's almost midnight. What do you think?" I let him hear the eye roll. "What are you up to?"

"Calling you."

He sounds lonely. It must be lonely to live by yourself. I guess I would know.

"Why don't you go to sleep?" I try to suppress my yawn, but it escapes despite my efforts.

"I'm not tired." Jordan lets out a heavy sigh. "Tell me a story."

"About what?"

"Anything."

I think for a moment. What can I possibly tell him a story about? I haven't done anything worth telling a story about in three years. I had an uneventful childhood; a normal high school experience and college was nothing exceptional. Until I met Gio. And he already knows Gio is dead.

"You already know my best stories." I say, breaking the silence.

"No, I don't." Jordan shuffles on the other end of the line. It sounds like he's rolling over in his own bed.

Petunia snores at my feet, and I pet her back with my left foot.

"Two months after Gio got sick," I finally begin, "he asked me if I wanted to get a dog. He said having a dog would help solidify our future together. As if living together and being together wasn't enough."

I hear Jordan breathe on the other end of the line.

"And he desperately wanted a French bulldog. So, for his birthday that year, I searched all over the city for a Frenchie. But Frenchies are just so expensive. And so I cut corners, and found a questionable breeder. She was two thousand dollars. And not a Frenchie."

Jordan laughs quietly.

"But she looks like she could be one, doesn't she?" I laugh in agreement.

"She doesn't look anything like a Frenchie, Rosemary," Jordan tells me.

I know. But Gio didn't. He was so delirious and tired from his treatments.

"If Gio ever noticed, he never told me."

"He was probably just happy you found him a dog."

"He probably was."

We've stayed quiet on the line for a few minutes, when Jordan finally speaks up.

"Do you miss him?"

"Sometimes, I do." *Do I miss Gio? Of course I do.*

"Just sometimes?"

"It's been a long time. I mostly miss having someone at all." *I'm finally admitingt it aloud.* It wasn't that foreign a thought to me, but to say it aloud was something else entirely. While I knew I would certainly outlive Gio, and I grieved him a little while he was still alive, I did the majority of my grieving after he died.

I had convinced myself he was the only person I could ever have, but finally my heart is opening up to the possibility that that isn't true. I miss having someone to love. Someone to hold, someone to kiss, someone to adore.

This isn't everything I am. I'm ready.

"I miss having someone to be with." I say into the phone, unsure if Jordan is still there.

"I'm with you, Ro," Jordan whispers, his voice light as a feather.

"Do you really mean that?" I ask, unsure whether or not to believe him.

"You know it."

As Jordan says that, I feel like I can really trust him. He's been there for me since I met him. *Almost.* The fall in the kitchen. The tea. The panic attack. *My crush is totally, full blown insane right now.*

"I miss having a person."

"I'll be your person."

"I'm not sure you wanna be my person."

"Thanks for the story, Ro. Goodnight."

"Goodnight."

Beep.

I had almost forgotten about it because of my panic attack over going on a date, but my crush on Jordan came back in a full force tsunami during the phone call. The way I see it, I face a choice: Confess. Or deny, deny, deny.

And deny, deny, deny I will. To Jordan, and to myself.

The second week of painting the mural has flown by, and as the day comes to a close, I'm getting antsier and antsier about my date. Jordan and I have spent the last few days bickering by day in the restaurant, but calling each other before we fell asleep at night, talking about our lives—and every day I learn new things about him.

He almost flunked ninth grade, but went to The Culinary Institute of America on full scholarship for culinary science.

He hates avocados. Nothing at The Red Kettle ever has avocado as an ingredient.

His umma is starting to forget her own children's names and he is considering hiring another chef so he can be at home with her more.

The renovations at the apartment will begin next month.

I tell him about group therapy. About the guys I match with on Tinder—but not about how they're there to distract me from him. About how I'm working on some other paintings in my free time to sell.

And when Friday rolls around, I'm wishing my date was with Jordan, not Rishi.

I've put my hair in a half up, half down style and wear a royal blue sweater with light wash jeans. I meet Rishi outside the restaurant, and when we go in, I instantly spot Jordan. He's making a beeline for the kitchen, his hands full with dishes. I'm proud of him for doing this mostly on his own.

Mae seats us at the same table as last time and delivers us towering glasses of iced water. Rishi and I do a proper cheers, and yet, all I can do is keep my eyes open for Jordan. He doesn't stop at our table this time and doesn't deliver our food.

Rishi is sweet and charming, but I am anything but fully enchanted. He's everything I want packaged in a nice body, but he's not *Jordan*. And I feel extraordinarily lousy for not paying more attention to him.

But all I can think is, where's Jordan? Will he bring us our water refills? I need to snap out of it. *You're on a date with someone else, don't be an asshole.* I shift my focus back to Rishi. He has ordered a sundubu jjigae, a tofu dish with fresh vegetables, and I have ordered a fresh take on arroz caldo, a chicken porridge, with a hard-boiled egg and slices of cucumber and lemon, on Mae's recommendation.

"So, where in the city do you live?" I ask Rishi, my feeble attempt to make conversation.

"Murray Hill."

"Oh, so do you work in finance?"

"Why does everyone think that?" Rishi's laughter is genuine, and my smile isn't forced. "I'm an art therapist actually. I work at the Children's Hospital."

"No wonder Jordan set us up—I'm a painter."

"I knew that already!" Rishi takes a huge, heaping bite of his tofu soup.

I flash back to my practice date with Jordan. *He doesn't talk with his mouth full.*

We chat throughout dinner. Rishi is twenty-seven, born in India, but moved here to attend NYU and medical school.

"How were you and Jordan college roommates if Jordan is a chef and you're a therapist?" The question comes to me suddenly.

"I wanted to be a pastry chef." Rishi smiles coyly. "I went to culinary school for a year. But my parents would never forgive me if I didn't become some kind of doctor. So I settled for a masters in art therapy."

"I totally understand. My parents wanted me to do literally anything but paint." My smiles are genuine now too. "Maybe you should bake something for me sometime."

"I'd love to! I keep trying to convince Jordan to open for breakfast so I can sell him my pastries."

"I'll see if I can help convince him."

"Speak of the devil." Rishi looks up as Jordan approaches our table, some kind of dessert loaf in his hand.

"Hey there, you guys." Jordan sets the plate down in front of us. "Complimentary dessert. This is the first time I've made it. Braided chocolate chili bread. It should be good, not too spicy." He gives a bashful smile and walks off before we can comment.

"Ladies first." Rishi cuts me a piece.

I'm hesitant to try it. My simple-minded, white girl alarm bells are ringing at the mention of *chili*. But how spicy could it be? Jordan said it wasn't too spicy, and he knows my palette. It's a chocolate dessert bread. It can't be that bad.

Oh, but it can be that bad.

The first bite I take I'm hit with a wall of hot, hot spice.

I can feel my eyes watering, my throat getting tight and the cough coming up in my chest. *What the fuck? I feel like I ate the world's hottest pepper whole.*

"I'm so sorry," I say through chokes and gulps of water, while Rishi just stares at me. Through big globs of tears, I watch him take a bite and have a similar reaction.

By the time I stop coughing, Rishi is in the full throes of his own. His face is totally pink, and it's clear he's having a hard time recovering.

I see Jordan standing over at the hostess station, watching Rishi and I cough our lungs up.

What's going on? Why's he just watching us? Did he do this on purpose?

With a tickle in my throat, I excuse myself from the table, and approach Jordan on behalf of Rishi.

"What's going on? Why did you give us something so spicy?" I gesture broadly to the restaurant, but hope he gets the idea I'm talking about the dessert. "It's clear you know Rishi doesn't like spicy food."

"Is it really that spicy?" Jordan asks, and it's obvious by the way the corners of his mouth pull at his falling face he knows what I'm talking about.

"Yes, it's really that spicy. You're going to tell me you didn't try it before bringing it out?" I'm beginning to get angry. *He knows it's not good. Why would he sabotage our dinner?*

"You're exaggerating."

"Stop lying to me, Jordan." I hiss, trying not to cause a scene. *Is he really going to pretend to not know?* "What's going on?"

"Okay, fine, I made it really spicy." Jordan grabs my shoulder and walks me into the hallway. "But only because I thought it would be funny."

"What? Why would you choose *now* to be funny?" He's very aware of the fact I'm trying to make up for my first atrocious date with Rishi.

"What Indian guy doesn't like spicy food?" Jordan's trying not to smile. "He's my old friend. It's fine."

"My date is not the time to be playing pranks on your roommate!" I'm furious. I wish I could roundhouse kick him in the face or at least shake him by the shoulders a little. "Did you ever think that this might ruin *my* date?"

This is not the considerate, attentive man I've come to know. "Clearly my expectations were too high." I break eye contact. I'm angry but I don't want to burn this bridge down to the ground.

Jordan doesn't have anything to say to me, other than, "I'm sorry, Rosemary," but I don't want to hear it. I'm feeling more upset than angry, and I'm perpetually worried I might cry. I take a huge, clown sized breath and hold it in. *Wait till you get home, or it won't just be Jordan ruining your date.*

I meet Rishi back at our table, and he's flushed in the face, mostly recovered.

"Hey," Rishi croaks out.

"So, I hear you don't like spicy food."

Rishi chokes out a beleaguered laugh. "No shit, Rosemary."

I crack a smile back at him, my face spiraling into something unrecognizable from a few moments ago. His frank response makes me think it'll be okay.

"Wanna get out of here?"

"Where did you have in mind?" I'm determined to not let Jordan ruin this date.

"A drink?"

"I don't drink, but as long as I can get a Shirly Temple, I'm happy." I'm confident I can salvage this.

"I think I can make that happen."

***

After taking me to his favorite dive-bar in the East Village, Rishi walks me to the front door of my apartment building. I feel content and happy. It's refreshing to have someone interested in me that isn't also my boss. There is no element of force or feign.

Standing on the stoop, Rishi takes my hand and pulls me softly, sauvely, into a goodbye kiss. *Flattering. But the butterflies aren't there.* By any standard, his kiss is perfect. Not forceful, not urgent, but it isn't until I picture Jordan being the one to kiss me, that I'm moved.

I break the kiss with a step backward and a bashful, "Thank you for everything," and go inside without so much as a goodbye, I'll text you! I hurriedly burst into the stairwell, feeling rotten, not being able to tell if I'm upset that I let another man kiss me that wasn't Gio—or Jordan.

For once, I climb the three flights of stairs up to my apartment, eager to wash away whatever feelings of loathing and despair and grief that might taint an otherwise good evening. Turning the corner of the hallway, I'm greeted by something unexpected at my doorstep.

A bouquet of white lilies?

Wrapped in delicate white paper tied with navy ribbon so silky, velvety, it's fabric too fancy for me to recognize, are ten angelic, blooming white lilies with dainty stems of white baby's breath. *Who are these from? And why?*

My first thought is my mother, but when I see the note card attached, I'm all too eager to tear it off, and have to force myself to gently untangle it from the ribbon tying it to the bouquet.

The note is in a matching navy envelope, about the size of a business card. Handwritten in pleasingly elegant cursive it reads: "I'll make it up to you. J."

That rat bastard. I can't be mad at him for too long even if I want to. Flowers?

I gingerly pick up the bouquet and unlock my front door. *He must have really gone through a lot to get these.* New York City might be the city that never sleeps, but flower shops still close, and to get them delivered within only a few hours? *He must have spent a fortune.*

The flowers really are gorgeous, and my heart is warmed. I'm not usually the type to forgive and forget when something is important to me, but the gesture is spoken for. The spicy dessert didn't *really*, *truly* ruin my date. It was a minor setback, if anything at all, and Rishi and I ended up having a great time away from The Red Kettle. But something sticks with me still. *Why would Jordan do that?* He was roommates with Rishi all those years ago and maintained the friendship this long.

He saw my struggle on my first date with Ethan and my first date with Rishi. He was normally kind, compassionate and sympathetic. *What in the world made him do that?*

The question irks me as I feed and walked Petunia. It bothers me while I shower and get ready for bed. It's completely out of character from everything I know about Jordan.

What would drive a man to act like that?

I can only think of a few things. Jordan's act of sabotage by making spicy chocolate bread when he knows his dear friend doesn't like spicy food is reminiscent of how a middle schooler acts when his friends are hanging out with other friends or how a dog growls when another dog gets too close to his own snack. *Is he jealous I was on a date with his friend?*

But he set us up!

And it finally clicks in my mind. He swiped right on me. He comforted me during my panic attack. He cooked for me and comped my meals at The Red Kettle. He took me on a practice date. The arms around me. Calling me by a nickname. The apology flowers.

Of course he's jealous. He likes me, too.

It's just be a matter of who will fess up first. And as the subordinate in this situation, I know it can't be me.

I feel incredibly pleased with myself for figuring this out. Like a scientist discovering a new element, I'm proud of my detective work. I'm too pleased to let my grief ruin this for me. For the first time in a long time, I have two men vying for my attention and I feel like a princess at the debutante ball.

I take my phone out and begin to wage the internal battle of who I should text first.

Rishi. Handsome enough to be a Gucci Model. Takes all my ups and downs in great spirits.

Jordan. Enough chemistry to blow fuses. Knows me more than I know myself.

And the decision is made for me when Jordan texts.

> Hey. I'm sorry for earlier. I don't know what came over me.

I giggle to myself. *I know what came over you. It has to be that you like me.* I snap a photo of the flowers on my countertop.

> All is forgiven.

> Promise?

> Promise.

I press the button to call Jordan, and he picks up on the first ring.

"Hey—" Jordan is ready to launch straight into an apology.

"Don't," I cut him off. "I forgive you. I'll chalk it up to a Neanderthal-man seeing his buddy for the first time in a while."

"That's not exactly true," he responds.

Of course it isn't!

"I didn't do it just to be funny."

Oh fuck. Is this happening now? Over the phone? I'm not ready.

"I really didn't know what I was thinking. I just really didn't want you to be on a date with him, Ro." His voice is solemn and more vulnerable than I've ever heard him speak. "But if you want to date him, you can."

I'm not ready. But I won't be a coward. I don't hang up the phone.

"What do you mean?" I ask him, nervous about the answer.

"I mean…" Jordan's voice trails off, almost silent.

And next thing I know, there's a beep in my ear.

That motherfucker hung up on me!

I call back. The phone rings for several minutes and goes straight to voicemail.

And turned his phone off. It feels extremely reminiscent of our first phone call. I debate going up to his apartment and knocking on his door, but I decide not to. *He made his bed, now he can lie in it. I'm not one to talk, either.* I've had a crush on this man almost since the moment I met him. He'll come to me when he's ready. I don't want to force it. Lord knows I'm still dealing with all of the grief and guilt that comes with having a dead fiancé.

I look at Petunia.

"What have we gotten ourselves into?"

Her response is a snort.

Chapter 12

That night, I dream of Gio. It's the same dream I have every time. It's pleasant, but nonsensical. It always starts like this:

He's dead.

And then all of the sudden, I get a text message from him. He's alive, he's *back*, and he's sorry he left me. He calls me and we talk a bit. I'm upset and angry he left me.

I am always asking: How could you scare me like that? How are you back? What did they do to bring you back? You weren't really dead at all?

He always gives me the same answer. They just thought he was dead and buried him alive. And after they realized their mistake, they brought him back up, and he was fine this whole time.

The dream transforms and I am curled up by his side again, holding his hand in a hospital bed like I should be, and he tells me how sorry he is for scaring me and sorry for leaving like that. By the time I forgive him for scaring me, the dream is over, and I am awake, alone, in my own home.

Every time I dream this, I feel like I offer a new generation of therapists ways to interpret craziness. *They don't bury bodies they think might have a chance of not being dead. That's not how this works. I know this.*

I wish I knew what it meant. And I probably never will.

I rub my temples in classic Rosemary fashion and try to think of an excuse to text Rishi. It's Saturday, and I want to invite him out. It's only natural since we had a good time yesterday. *He will expect a text from me anyway.* And if I don't distract myself with Rishi, I will surely distract myself with Jordan.

Jordan. I have not heard from him since he hung up on me, and I am not about to be the one to reach out first. Because I know the words that would come tumbling out of my mouth would be ones I would be sure to regret before I finished the mural. The fact he said he didn't want me to go out with Rishi made me even angrier and made me want to go out with Rishi out of spite.

I glance at the lilies on my countertop. They stare back at me, their beauty unflinching. *Fuck that.* Rishi…

Want to go to the Farmers' Market this morning?

I'll meet you outside your building in 20.

In my mind, I look lascivious, almost pornographic, but the outfit I select comes off as horny preteen in the mall. I opt for a delicate, strappy one shoulder top and my classic denim mom jeans. It definitely gives a: "holding a bouquet of flowers at the farmers market" type of vibe, and not, "I want to kiss my neighbor who I'm angry with." I dab blush on my cheeks and mascara on my lashes. *I really am going for preteen at the mall, huh?*

Petunia looks up at me with her big bug-eyed face.

Mind if I bring my dog?

Fine by me.

I suit up Petunia in her harness and tie a floral bandana around her neck, and with a kiss on the top of her head, we are out the door. I forget to say my prayer, and my regret is instantaneous.

Jordan is in the lobby.

I try to walk past him without him noticing, but Petunia gives me away. She's excited to see him.

"Where are you two going?" he asks, thumbing through the mail, clearly eyeing my out-of-the-ordinary outfit.

"Just for a walk." *I'm trying to avoid this conversation; doesn't he get that?*

"Dressed like that?"

He does get it.

Rishi appears in the building doorway, waving like a flag on a dock, but thankfully waits outside and doesn't come in. *Goddamnit.* He catches Jordan's attention.

"I suppose he's not here to see me." Jordan grimaces, the displeasure drips off his voice like honey on a hot spoon.

"We're going to the farmers' market."

"Good luck with that," Jordan says plainly, as if I'd said, "I'm going to jury duty!" His eyes are daggers, but mine are assault rifles.

I pick up Petunia and stomp out the door. *Two can play at this bullshit game.*

Rishi and I walk the farmers' market awkwardly, like two teenagers who know their parents are watching. We make awkward conversation with awkward gestures, and I know it's because my heart is back in the apartment building, arguing with Jordan in the lobby.

I'm standing in front of a bouquet of lavender when Rishi offers to buy it for me, and without thinking, I decline faster than he asked, saying that Jordan bought me flowers last night.

"Jordan bought you flowers last night?" he asks, presumptuous.

This date isn't going to end in a fairytale kiss.

"Rosemary," Rishi starts, his hands folded in front of him like he's giving a presentation. "I'm having a great time with you. But I think you're going out with the wrong guy."

Fuck. Is it really that obvious?

My mind immediately jumps to Jordan. "Did you say anything to him?"

Rishi gives me a cool laugh. "No. You have to be the one to tell him. Let me know if you change your mind."

I walk home instead of taking the subway.

***

I suck it up and dial Jordan's number.

"Hello?" The familiar crackle.

"It's me."

"I know it's you."

"What are you doing right now?".

"Rosemary." His voice is a sunken ship.

"Yeah?" I'm an anchor.

"Can you come up here?"

The offer is incredibly tempting, and while my brain is saying, *No! You'll do bad things!* I hear myself saying, "Yes, I'll be there in five minutes."

I quickly change out of my *fuck me* outfit and put on the fuzziest pink bathrobe over the rattiest T-shirt I can find, and after locking my front door, I begin climbing the two flights up the stairs, and round the corner to my old—Jordan's—apartment. That still takes some getting used to.

He opens the door, and I see him standing there, looking delicious in a black turtleneck with equally black jeans. *I am in a fluffy pink bathrobe.*

I'm caught off guard by him once again. His eyes are almost as black as his outfit and I'm fluttering at the thought. I am slightly out of breath, and Jordan's face is flushed a light pink. I wonder if he's been drinking.

"Are you okay? Did you climb the stairs?" he asks.

"I did. I was in a hurry,"

"Why are you in such a rush? It's not like I'm going anywhere." He laughs at my absurdity.

"Can I come in?" I ask timidly. He opens the door wider to gesture me in.

"I can get you some water." Jordan swallows hard.

He hands me a glass of water that I eagerly chug down.

"Rosemary…I need to tell you, Rosemary, that I…" He says my name like a curse. "You can't have dates at The Red Kettle anymore." He spits out the words like poison.

"Where's this coming from?" I ask. I trail off and look at my feet.

"I can't let this go on longer," Jordan says. His face looks like I'm the one who's given him bad news. I cross my arms and turn away from him, toward the kitchen counter.

"Why not?" I mumble, my hands automatically going through my hair to my temples. "I mean, I understand…Did something change?"

I look Jordan in the eye, and he stares back at me with a look I haven't seen before because I am so used to the look that precludes it. *Play dumb.*

He has the laser focus of someone aiming a gun at a target when he takes a step towards me. We are two countries warring over the same piece of land.

I am the heavily armed opponent, my guns aimed directly at his heart, his aimed directly at mine. He is a silent sharpshooter, his hands are the weapon of choice. They remain chivalrously by his side.

My hands are my weapon of choice, and they are reaching beyond my level.

We both know where this is going and have imagined this scenario a thousand different times in the ways we have wanted, but not done. It is a ferocious, endless battle to fight any instinct I have to touch him.

It could have been in the restaurant.

It could have been in the park.

It could have been last night, or the night before, or any other night since the very first night.

Jordan quietly takes a second step.

A third. A fourth. A fifth.

Until he's close enough to touch me.

We argue silently, debating how this should go down. Who will pull the trigger first? Will either of us surrender?

Me? Or you?

Who will break first?

It's him. He shoots first with a sweep of his fingers on the side of my face and a quiet whisper of my name. "Rosemary."

My defenses are falling. His voice is like the softest dress of silk chiffon, buttery and rich. Jordan's fingers travel through my hair, to take the place of my own hands on my temples. I am the buttery dress in his hands.

We move slowly like molasses, both of us trying to delay the inevitable because there's something so sweet, so tempting about the just about to, not quite there, the almost time. There's something so genuinely despicable about making me wait this long.

I fire a second shot—I put a hand on his chest. *Who's in charge now?*

It's the first time I've ever touched Jordan like this, like someone with intentions, like someone with an agenda. His chest is firm muscle under the knit fabric of his sweater. Everything about it makes me want to lay down all my weapons and let him shoot bullets through me.

"Rosemary," Jordan whispers, his voice a steady battle drum.

A third shot. One more hand. I put my other hand on his waist, squeezing his hip bone. I weather the fury of his fire as he rubs my temple in slow, soft circles. I am almost beaten down, on the brink of surrender.

"I can't get the thought of you and him out of my head."

Me and Rishi.

"What do you mean?"

Is he jealous?

"You can't go out with him anymore."

"I don't ask who you've been going out with."

"I haven't been going out with anyone since I met you."

Confess. Confess.

We are staring into each other's eyes, analyzing like we have done so many times before. And before I can unload my weapons and surrender once and for all, he asks.

"Can I kiss you?"

Sweet, tender victory. "You can do whatever you want, Jordan."

I confirm his loss by brushing his lips with my very own personal atom bomb. *I kissed him first.* And as it turns out, I am, by far, the winner of this long-fought battle. His kisses are the homecoming parade I have so desperately wanted. He is a lightning bolt, quick and hot. A kiss here. And there. The side of my face. A nip of my neck.

And I am blown to bits, regardless of my battle victory. I find myself kissing him back with such ferocity, I can't catch my breath. I'm spewing hot lava like a volcano.

Jordan gives me a taste of his tongue and I abandon my own ships for the other side. He pulls me thoroughly into his own arms, wrapping me tightly in a bouquet of his warmth. I rampage over him like a hurricane over the shore.

He is the lighthouse, now.

This isn't like the kiss from Rishi last night. This is needy and destitute. This is prying me open. With each kiss, we are two continents colliding, creating earthquakes everywhere we touch.

I'm ready to accept your confession now, Jordan. Am I?

I grow hesitant with my response, and I jolt back like I was shocked with an electric buzzer.

"Oh my god. I'm so sorry."

What have I done? What did I just do?

Jordan stands there stunned, his hands releasing me just as fast, going up to his mouth like he can't believe what he just did either.

I feel a bloodthirsty wave of grief come over me. It looms over me like a comically evil villain, waiting to catch me when I'm down, itching to snatch me up and tear me limb from limb. *Oh my god. I just made out with someone else.* I stave it off for fear of crying.

Instead of crying, I just laugh. *I'm laughing. This is fucking hysterical. But oh my god, I missed it so much. I missed being kissed. I just want to kiss him again.*

Jordan still stands there, dumbfounded.

"What?" he asks, his voice flustered, like I had just embarrassed him instead of myself.

"I'm so sorry." I double over and flap my hands at him. "This was a mistake." I turn towards the door to leave and bury myself under a pile of weighted blankets, but he reaches and yanks my arm to furl me towards him.

"It wasn't a mistake to me, Rosemary."

I'm forced to stare at his eyes. They are not peaceful.

"I...I..." I'm taken aback. He really had meant to kiss me.

"This isn't a joke to me."

"This isn't a joke to me either!" I'm hurling my words at him. Tearing my eyes away from him is an act of violence.

"Rosemary." The moment he says my name, I release my vigor and let him pull me close again. He puts a gentle, giant hand on my chin and brings my face to look up at him. I look at him, completely doe-eyed. *He is so fucking attractive right now.* I somehow manage not to shove my tongue down his throat.

"I like you. Jordan. Like, I really like you." My confession is an act of terrorism.

"I like you too, Rosemary. I think we should try this."

He knows how nervous I am to try this.

"You don't have to say anything."

And I don't. I just kiss him again before weaving my way out of his arms and leaving just as abruptly as I came.

Chapter 13

I stumble out into the hallway, feeling like the worst possible version of myself.

Now, I let my tears fall. I wish I hadn't left, and like some kind of idiot, I press the down button for the elevator instead of just taking the stairs. *Because I am some kind of idiot. And I hope Jordan will come after me.*

He does.

Jordan opens his door and peers into the hallway, watching me let my tears out like some kind of depraved orphan child getting a slice of bread for the first time in her life.

"Come back here, Rosemary," he says from the doorway.

The elevator arrives and the doors open and close, but I don't move.

"Please come back over here," Jordan asks. "I won't make you, but I won't ask again."

I turn around as if on cue, and march over to him, tears bubbling in my eyes like a fountain at the mall. *Like I could stay away even if I wanted to.*

"What's the matter?" Jordan whispers quietly. He reaches for my face, using the pads of his thumbs to wipe my tears.

"What do you think?" I retort. I'm colder than ice.

"Was it really that bad?"

I bark out a laugh through boogers and hot tears. "No."

"This is a first for me, you know." Jordan sounds like he's lecturing a classroom of rowdy kindergarteners. "I've never made a girl cry after just kissing her."

"I've never cried after kissing a man, either. So we're in the same boat." I wipe my nose on my ridiculously giant robe sleeve, wishing I had a tissue or a paper towel or a wad of toilet paper. *Actually, I have cried after kissing a man. Gio.*

"What's on your mind, Rosemary?" Jordan ushers me back into the apartment, and I'm not sure if I can take being back in this place after kissing a man who wasn't Gio in it. I am a belligerent wild pony, walking all over the place, and Jordan puts an arm around me, corralling me to the couch.

"I don't think I can be in this apartment and not fucking lose it," I say flatly. I look Jordan in the eyes. "I was engaged to another man in here." I laugh at my absurdity, the tears beginning again after a brief moment.

Jordan doesn't say anything, he looks at me like my therapist does, as if to say, welcome to my office, please take a seat on my couch. "And?"

I don't know how to explain to him I cannot be in here with him.

"I have too much history here."

"Do you?"

Do I? I lived here far longer without Gio than I ever did with him.

"I grieved here."

"Does that make it unlivable?" Jordan asks me. I don't know how he manages to ask the right things.

"Is it bad if it does?" I look at him solemnly. "I don't think I can ever look at this place again without thinking of Gio and all of the time I spent crying and being miserable and having panic attacks."

I've never told Jordan what happened to Gio. "We lived together here for a year, and we were supposed to get married that fall."

Jordan wraps me in a hug while I tell him about my fiancé.

"He had a seizure in September. He had no history of seizures. They did scans and tests. It was brain cancer." I take a black-hole sized pause. "Totally incurable. There was nothing to be done except wait it out."

Quiet, gentle tears roll down my cheeks. *I have told this story a thousand times, and surely, I will tell it a thousand more. What is one more time?*

"They buried him in December in his hometown in Texas. I went to the funeral. I haven't been back."

"Why not?" Jordan asks me gently.

"I couldn't bear it."

He rubs my shoulders and I put a hand up to my temple, holding my head low.

"I didn't like seeing him like that. I don't want my last memory of him to be a stone in the ground."

"Thank you for telling me that, Rosemary." Jordan lifts my legs over his own, and cradles me in his lap like the massive baby I am. "You don't have to carry it all, you know?"

"What do you mean?"

"Don't underestimate yourself," Jordan tells the top of my head. *He really is a massive, giant of a man.* I feel like a teeny, tiny cookie crumb in his warm arms. "You act like no one will ever be interested in you because of your past."

"That's usually the case."

"Rosemary. Is that really the case? You just went on two dates!" Jordan laughs into my hair.

I think for a moment. *Is that really the case?*

"Maybe that was the case a year or two ago. But that's certainly not the case now." Jordan rests his chin on top of my head.

"And there's me." He laughs. "I am so interested in you."

"You're only interested in me when something embarrassing happens," I say, the cynic in me leaking through every orifice of my body.

Jordan presses a kiss to the top of my head. He shifts to stand up, and I stand up with him.

"Okay, enough of this." He turns me to face him and takes my tiny mouse hands in his. I feel like a pouting child in his arms. "Have a little confidence in yourself, Ro. You haven't scared me off yet."

I look up at him, my eyes red and puffy.

"Let me make this clear to you, Rosemary." Jordan stares directly to my soul, my heart, whatever internal organ he can lay his eyes on. "I'm interested in you. Your past is included in that. I don't care that you have a dead fiancé. I don't care if you cry. I like you for you. Tears and all."

I feebly smile back at him.

"I bet you'll live to regret saying that." *I hope he's telling the truth.*

He grins back at me, fiercer than ever.

"I'll count on it."

Jordan takes my hand, and walks me out of his apartment, down the stairs and into my own. Petunia skitters around our ankles. He presses an unassuming kiss to my forehead.

"Go out with me."

How can he have so few reservations after I bawled my eyes out on his sofa?

"Tomorrow night. 6:00 p.m. Come to The Red Kettle."

"What about the dinner service?" I ask.

"I'll close the restaurant early."

"What? Are you crazy?"

"Probably." Jordan gives me a mellow grin.

He doesn't mind.

"Just come. Promise me you'll come."

"I'll be there."

That afternoon, I'm in my head and I know it. *I am fucking crazy. What have I done?* I replay the morning in my head. Our kiss. And how much I wanted it. The especially fucked up thing about grief is that it mangles your perception of yourself so badly, you forget you're a human too.

You feel like a fake and a fraud. How dare you want to love again?

You convince yourself you're not funny and charming. You're cringey and embarrassing.

You're definitely not sweet and endearing. You're clingy and overbearing.

Your old self is on some far off pedestal, far beyond any reasonable reach, but still, you desperately reach and grab and clutch onto whatever pieces you can get. The statue of your old self is chipped away by every sunrise and sunset, and there is nothing you can do but watch it get whipped to pieces in the wind.

You are a self-fulfilled prophecy. You are everything you don't want to be.

But how could you not be? Your life is turned upside down in a single phone call.

I make sure everyone knows, all the time, as evident when Jordan found me crying in the hall. *But it didn't turn him away. In fact, it just made him chase me more.*

Maybe he's the one fucked in the head.

The thing I miss the most about Jordan's apartment was the

balcony. This apartment doesn't have one. If I want fresh air, the best I can do is stick my head out the window by the fire escape. Sitting on the fire escape feels a little risky—and technically illegal.

Is it too soon to call Jordan again? It was less than two hours since I saw him, but all I want to do was talk to him about this. Even so, it's probably best to let it lie. Meaning…if I saw him again, I would certainly try to kiss him. Even I'm smart enough to see that.

Hours pass and I don't know how I manage. I ask myself a thousand questions, not knowing the answer to a single one and too afraid to find out. A million thoughts plow their way through the wrinkles in my brain.

What will I tell my parents? What will I tell Gio's parents? The support group?

Does this mean I have to take down the photos of Gio?

Do I have to get rid of Gio's things?

I laugh at the ridiculous thought of having to get rid of Petunia simply because she also belonged to Gio. But it is a fine line to walk, and I don't know the answers. If I date someone new, what do I do with all the evidence I was in another relationship I doesn't willingly exit? Who decides?

Me, I think.

I will not scrub the evidence that Gio and I were together from the universe. I've worked so hard to keep it here. *Why would I want to get rid of it?*

I think back to what Melissa said to me. You move forward, not on.

When you move forward, it doesn't mean you erase all the things that you leave behind. My grief, my sorrow and all my pain make up who I am today. The me who was grieving in the past is still somewhere within the me who is desperately trying so hard to be happy today.

You and I are not so different after all.

I don't know why it took me so long to understand that, when it seemingly took Jordan only a few minutes. *Maybe it's different when it's your reality.*

I think it plainly. I am afraid that loving someone new means I won't love Gio anymore. I love Gio through giving someone new my love.

Which begs the question: Is Jordan the one I want to give my love to?

And when I am in bed later that night, itching to call him, I have my answer when my phone rings and his name pops up on the screen. My heart skips forty beats and the butterflies in my stomach climb to my throat.

"Hello?"

"Hey, Ro," Jordan murmurs, his voice quiet and hoarse on the other end of the line.

"Why are you calling me?" I ask, trying not to sound too desperate for an answer. I'd been waiting all afternoon for this very moment.

"I call you every night at this time."

"I guess you do." He's not wrong. I don't even know why I asked that.

"I was just thinking about you."

"What about me?" *He was thinking about me.* The butterflies multiply by six hundred.

"How beautiful you looked today."

I blush even though he can't see me.

"That top was ridiculously attractive. I don't understand how you looked so good in it. I can't wrap my head around you, Rosemary." Jordan's normally perky and bouncy voice is dreamy and ambrosial.

I don't even know what to say. It's been so long since I've flirted without looking like a total dork. I stay silent on the line, but place the phone near my face so my breathing is near the mic so he can tell I'm still listening.

"It doesn't hurt hearing that," I tease him. "Thanks for the ego boost."

"Please. Your ego needs it, frankly." Jordan laughs lightly on the other end of the line, and I hear him shuffling.

"Where are you?"

"I just got into bed."

"I'm already in bed," I answer, talking faster than I mean to for fear of spilling the coalition of heinously dirty thoughts barging into my mind like I'm fifteen and discovering that guys are like, kind of hot, actually.

"What are you wearing now?" Jordan's voice is softer than velvet and sultrier than a little black dress.

"I feel like a phone sex operator answering that." I giggle like a maniac, like a little girl in a candy store.

"Is that so bad? I bet it pays well."

"What are you wearing?" I flip the question on Jordan. "Wait, I take that back. I don't want to know."

I don't want to know so badly, because once I know, I won't be able to stop thinking about it.

I picture Jordan in his fictional California king bed, sprawled in a jungle of bamboo linens, and I am immediately flustered because that is surely the situation right now.

"Why not?" It's Jordan's turn to giggle and it sounds ridiculously cute coming from a grown man's body.

"It's none of my business," I answer matter-of-factly. *I desperately want it to be my business.* "But you don't strike me as a flannel pajama pants kind of guy."

"You'd be right about that." Jordan gives me a taste of his golden laugh again.

What kind of guy is he then? I wonder if he's a briefs or boxers guy.

"Only for matching family photos on Christmas morning."

"You do strike me as that kind of person." I'm grinning ear to ear. "Especially when it's for next year's holiday card."

"Oh, you know it. I have three sisters and a niece. It's matching pajamas or death."

"You would know."

"Do you have any siblings?" Jordan's voice lowers as he asks me.

"I don't. It's just me." I let out a somber sigh. "My parents moved to North Carolina when they retired."

"You didn't want to go with them?" Jordan asks.

"I couldn't leave the city. Because of Gio, partly. And partly because I love this place too much."

"What's your favorite part of the city?" Jordan asks me, a relentless list of questions coming out of his mouth.

"Is it bad if it's a cliché answer?" I'm decisive.

"Yes, it's bad! You fake New Yorker, you."

"My favorite place is Central Park."

Jordan shames me with a vapid *tsk* saying I should know better.

"I can't help it. When I was ten years old, before I moved here, it was the first place we visited. And the moment I entered the park, I knew it was my dream to move here and be a painter."

"All right, all right. I'll accept that answer but only because of the childhood backstory."

I laugh. "You'd have to accept it no matter what, because that's the answer."

We talk late into the night as usual, like there was no fiery kiss between us, and by the time midnight rolls around, I am falling asleep.

"Jordan," I say, my voice a secret. "Do you want to know something?" I am dazed by sleep.

"Sure, Rosemary, I always want to know."

"I wish I could kiss you in my bed. But if you came here, I don't think I could contain myself."

"I would be beside myself to be there, Rosemary, but I don't think I could contain myself either." Jordan's words echo through my chest cavity to crush and squeeze my heart, artery by artery, capillary by capillary. *He really feels the same way.*

I throw it all out there.

"How did you know you liked me?" I ask.

"When I told you not to do something, and then you did it anyway."

The kitchen.

"You were practically begging me to come in there."

"I was not." Jordan's laugh is stubborn and a stump in the ground. "You really should wear non-slip shoes." Jordan's voice switches to serious.

"Will you let me in the kitchen tomorrow?" I beg him.

"Only if you wear non-slip shoes."

"What if I don't?" I tease.

"Then you can't come in."

"Or you'll have to carry me."

The thought of his arms around me again was dazzling. I would melt into them like a popsicle in the sun. He would have no choice in the matter. I almost think better of it, but I say, "I can't wait to get my hands on you again."

"Whoa there, slow down, I think we ought to take it down a notch."

Jordan is lying through his motherfuckin' teeth, but I lay there and agree with him.

"Too hot."

"Maybe you're right."

Maybe he is right. I did cry after a single makeout sesh like a total pansy.

"You'll have plenty of other opportunities later. One day at a time, Ro."

"One day at a time," I sleepily agree.

"Go to sleep now," he commands.

I am an obedient puppy.

"Goodnight now." I hang up the phone, and roll over.

One day at a time.

This could be mine every night, but I have to be brave enough to take it.

Chapter 19

That night, it's more of the same.

I dream of Gio.

It starts the same as every dream I have of Gio. Pleasant. Nonsensical. He's dead. He's alive, *he's back*. And he's still sorry he left me. He wants to get back together.

But this dream is different.

Jordan is there and he's saying: "Choose. Me or him."

And dream me can't stand the thought of losing Jordan now. I've already lost Gio. But Jordan, too? *Unbearable.*

I choose Jordan. I just got him; how could I lose him already? *I won't lose him.*

Dream Jordan is thrilled. He wraps his arms around me, and Gio begins fading away like the memory he is. *I am in the present, I am in the present, I am in the present.*

I wake up in a cold sweat. It's the first time that dream has ever turned into anything more than me being upset with Gio for leaving. Like the sun over the river, it truly dawns on me that we never find our way back to loving the same way twice.

This is it. So much of grief is arguing with yourself.

This is my choice and my chance. My love for Gio is remade, reborn and restained into something fiery and new for someone else. I have to choose Jordan; I think to myself.

Petunia and I bask in the sunshine streaming in between the

curtains. I've spent the better part of three years being sad, and I'm scared that I'm permanently impaired at this point, but I pet Petunia's pouty face, and announce to her, "This is it. I can do it. I'm brave enough."

That afternoon, I work on my painting of Jordan. I paint the twinkles of stars in the sky you'd never see in New York City, the steam of a bubbling pot, the wrinkles in a white cotton shirt. I step back and look at the painting.

It is a love letter to everything I know about him. I might not be good with words from my brain to my tongue, but at least I can paint a pretty picture of everything that goes on inside my head. I add highlights in his hair, shadows on the brick wall and sign it with a looping, swooping R and O.

I carefully take the wet painting off the easel, and when it's dry in two to three weeks, I'll give it to him. His oil painting, made with my own oil paints and feelings buried deep inside the colors. It's nearing four o'clock and I know Jordan will be here soon to walk me to The Red Kettle.

Getting ready is agonizing. I'm looking forward to seeing him—but I feel frumpy in the yellow sundress I planned on wearing, and I'm desperate to find something that makes my outsides feel as good as my inside. I've worn sweats and ratty T-shirts for so long, any clothes that require actual matching and putting together make me feel out-of-place and homely. I switch to a marled periwinkle pull over sweater with jeans and chunky sneakers and hope for the best.

By the time 4:30 rolls around and there's a sharp knock on my door, I am barely ready. Cheeks red from blush or embarrassment, who knows, I undo the chain lock and peek through the crack before opening it fully.

We stand in the doorway like two courting teenagers on their first date to the Cracker Barrel, our parents eyeing us from two tables away. We both open and close our mouths like we have something to say, but no words come out.

"You're something else, Rosemary." Jordan looks like he wants to whistle and is struggling to keep it in. He looks me up and down, and I let him.

Meanwhile, Jordan is something else, himself.

His black hair is swept off his face by a pair of square Ray-Bans atop his head, and a red corduroy button up makes his brown eyes look especially golden brown, like cookie butter. There is simply no way to describe them other than *delicious*. His form-fitting jeans make me swoon in a way that's totally inappropriate for the type of date we are about to go on.

I want to unzip his skin and climb inside like some kind of freak. I beg my brain not to say that aloud.

"You're one to talk."

"Ready?" he asks.

"One sec." I step out and lock the door behind me. "I didn't know you did pick-up and drop-off service." *Is it normal for your date to meet you at your door?*

"Only for those who deserve it."

We walk out of the building arm in arm, and I feel like I'm being walked to the prom. The only thing I'm missing is the corsage on my wrist. Getting on the train feels like something out of a romantic comedy and I can hardly contain myself.

I sit in the only empty seat, and Jordan hangs onto the bar above my head, his chiseled torso approximately at my eye level. I just want to be at the restaurant, sitting on Jordan's lap. *What has gotten into me?* Every time I think of something suggestive, I act so surprised at myself, unable to believe I'm capable of such dirty thoughts. *But is it really that far-fetched for a grown woman to think about a crush?*

The train flies by the two stops and we walk so fast, it feels like Jordan has essentially teleported me from my apartment to the restaurant. The restaurant is dark, and Jordan carefully seats me at the single set table. He lights candlesticks on a brass candelabra on either end of the bar I never noticed before. He lights two more attached to the wall, and then disappears into the kitchen.

I am exalted. *Is all of this just for me?*

It is.

Jordan emerges with two orange cocktails that he describes as Italian Blood Orange Soda but without the cream.

"And with no alcohol," he confirms after I ask.

I gingerly take a sip and confirm for myself.

It's delicious. I smile up at him, and he clasps his hands as if he were my waiter, and then backtracks into the kitchen, and I giggle at the sight of him doing a light skip through the door. I can't wait to see what he's cooked up for us. Surely it's going to be fantastic. So I'm surprised when he emerges with a large tray, a bowl of meat and several dozen dumpling wrappers.

When I question what's going on, all he says is, "Don't over flour, don't overfill and you'll be good." Jordan mocks up a simple wrap up for me, a simple method where you pinch the ends of the dough together in the center, and then on either side. Then, you bring the ends of your semi-circle together to form a little round ball with a divot in the center. *Seems easy enough.*

I give it a go, and while a little haphazardly done, Jordan gives it a smile of approval. He works on other complicated techniques involving complicated pinching and twisting of dough. I have never felt so clumsy with my hands.

"Is this how you felt when I tried to show you how to paint?" I ask, holding up a disaster of a dumpling. He made it look so easy, but I'm struggling still.

"Yes, almost exactly." Jordan smiles bashfully. He stands up and walks around to where I'm sitting opposite him. "Let me show you."

He spoons a clump of meat into a fresh wrapper and lifts it onto my cutting board. "Put your hands here." He shows me where to put my hands, just barely holding onto the pliable dough. Placing his hands over mine, covered in flour, he goes through the motions while I feel like just a distraction under his hands.

"Don't pinch too hard," he instructs. "Got it?"

"Got it."

"Bring the ends to meet in the middle."

"Meet in the middle?"

"Meet in the middle."

He places a perfectly, well done dumpling on the tray. I spoon myself a lump of meat into a new wrapper, trying to follow what he told me. *Pinch. Pinch. Pinch. Meet in the middle.*

I hold up a marginally better dumpling.

"Not bad, Ro," he laughs. "Now, I'll do the rest."

"I think that's for the best."

I sip on my drink, intently watching Jordan fold dumplings in intricate patterns I could only ever paint.

"Who taught you how to do these?"

"YouTube." Jordan barks out a laugh.

"Really? Not an old, family secret?"

"Maybe starting now it will be." Jordan winks. "What kind of shoes are you wearing? Are they non-slip?"

I bring a foot up to show him my sandals. "I don't think so?"

"Just promise me you'll be careful."

"I promise.'

We carefully walk into the kitchen, where Jordan has a bubbling fryer already popping with oil. He carefully drops about half the dumplings into the vat and then walks me over to the stove.

"I'm going to pan fry these. They'll be crispy on the bottom but soft on the top, yeah?" He looks at me for approval.

"Sounds good to me." I smile. "Fried anything sounds good to me, if I'm being honest."

Jordan goes back and forth between the fryer and the pan, like the true line cook he is, while I stand behind the large commercial kitchen style island counter in front of the stoves. He banished me there after he turned the stoves on, for fear I might set myself on fire.

He gives me two large pearlescent white plates and directs me over to a refrigerator where there's an already dressed cranberry arugula salad waiting. I use a massive pair of tongs to place heaps of salad onto each plate.

This date just feels like hanging out. And I'm glad for it. I don't think I could handle the pressure of a real date. Getting dressed up. Going to a fancy restaurant. Having to talk about myself. Deciding who pays. Having something to do with my hands has taken my mind off my anxiety about the fact I'm on a date.

Maybe it's on purpose. And if it is, Jordan sure has good intuition. I try not to psych myself out as he places perfectly fried dumplings on each plate. We each take one and make our way back to the dining room. Jordan takes a pitcher from behind the bar and refreshes our drinks without me even asking.

When he sits down opposite me, I ask, "Food is kinda how you show love, isn't it?"

I thought he would falter at my use of *love* but he doesn't hesitate, not even for a minute.

"Yeah. It kinda is." We do a *cheers* with our dumplings instead of our drinks.

"What's your favorite dish to make?" I ask, violating Jordan's rule on not talking with your mouth full.

"Dumplings." Jordan grins through a stuffed mouth. "Even though they're not on my usual menu."

We eat and chat and I feel at peace. *This is the kind of date I was meant for.* I'm not worried about what happened with Ethan or Rishi. I feel like he knows me so well already. There's no crowded, bustling restaurant. There's no pressure to get to know him in ninety minutes or less.

It's just two friends, and some fried dumplings. What more could a girl want?

"Are we friends?" I ask suddenly.

"Of course," Jordan answers. "Why wouldn't we be?"

"Because of what happened." My totally sudden kiss and then running away like some kind of freak.

"I'm always your friend, Rosemary," Jordan tells me, shifting in his chair from across the table. "I'm your friend first. That hasn't changed."

"I don't want that to change. You've been a good friend to me."

"Then it won't change." Jordan looks disappointed for a brief moment, but his face changes quickly when he realizes I've noticed.

I want to be more than just friends. But I don't want to lose you entirely in the process.

"Unless you want it to," Jordan adds at the last second, before I'm about to say I should probably be heading out.

"We should just stay friends, I think," I say, biting my tongue. I want to be more than just friends so badly. "I do have some grief stuff to figure out, I guess." I am not sure of my words in the slightest.

"Yeah. You do have that stuff to figure out," Jordan confirms with me.

"I don't want to do anything I'll regret." I bite my tongue as soon as I say it. *I regret implying that I'd regret you.*

"I get it, Ro." Jordan stacks our empty plates together. "Let me take you home."

I'm not ready for this to be over.

"Sure."

I don't want to go home.

Riding the train feels like an act of betrayal. Jordan is clearly disappointed with my statement of being *just friends*. I almost feel bad for him. I know how badly I want to be more than friends. It's such a big feeling, and I don't know how to handle it.

By the time we reach my apartment door, I am feeling terrible about shutting him down so quickly. *This wasn't a practice date. It was a real date.* I flash back to him saying he'd kiss me after a real date, but the kiss never comes. *You idiot! You were the one who told him you wanted to be just friends!*

"Do you want to come in for a drink?" I stall. "Tea? Coffee?" I don't even have any coffee. "Please. Just come in for a moment and say hello to Petunia."

When he doesn't say anything, I just unlock my door and Jordan follows me in. Petunia greets us like a silly little clown, paw over paw in the doorway, and there's a smile on Jordan's face as he coos at her like the little baby she is.

I put the kettle on and get two mugs out of the cabinet while Jordan walks over to the window where I have my painting station set up.

"It's not quite as big as the studio in the old apartment, but it works," I tell him, as he flips through some of the sketches I left out.

I'm turning to pour hot water when I hear him ask, "What's this?"

Ah, fuck. It's the painting of him.

"It's a gift." I swallow my pride. "It's for you."

He studies it for a moment, his face unsure what to make of what he's taking in.

"Who is that?" he asks.

"It's you."

"This is gorgeous, Rosemary."

"You're just saying that."

He asks me a string of questions and I don't get a chance to answer any of them before he asks another. "How long did this take you? Why me? Did you do this all by yourself?"

"Two weeks. Yes, I did this by myself."

I don't answer why I chose to paint Jordan. *It's because I couldn't stop thinking about him.* He sets the painting down back where he found it and puts me on the spot again.

"Why'd you paint me, though? We barely knew each other when you started this."

I take a heaping gulp of air. How do I answer this without making it seem like I'm a creep?

The grin on his face tells me everything I need to know. He's putting two and two together from my silence. "Why'd you paint me, Rosemary?" Jordan's voice is sing-songy as if he's caught me in some bad act.

"Why do you think, Jordan?" I return his vivacious smile. *I can put him on the spot too.*

He swiftly, unexpectedly pulls me into his arms, and I am the one in the hot seat again.

"Be honest with me, Rosemary." I shudder as he presses a hand into the small of my back, the other hand traveling up my neck to the back of my head, tousling my hair in a way that suggests less like, *you young scamp, you!* and more like, *so fucking sexy.* "Why'd you paint me?"

When his eyes meet mine, I have no choice but to answer honestly. I try to make it clear that all I've been doing since yesterday is yearning for the sweetness of his lips and the cradle of his arms.

"Don't be cruel, Rosemary. Tell me."

"I couldn't stop thinking about you."

I can't tell if he's satisfied with my answer, because his face doesn't change. The only thing that changes is that his grip on my neck tightens, and I could easily be brainwashed into killing for this man. There is no way I could break free from his grip, even if I wanted to, but *I don't.*

"I need you to kiss me," I command him.

"I couldn't stop thinking about you either, Rosemary." Jordan's face is wickedly close to mine, and if he weren't holding my neck, I'd crane closer and kiss him like I was on fire. But he has a hold on me. "But I want you to be sure before we go any further."

I'm sure, I think to myself. "I'm sure." I say aloud to him, willing him with my mind to touch me anywhere besides my neck and back.

"Are you, Ro?" Jordan's eyes are conniving thieves, draining my energy with them. This is almost as good as any kiss. I am completely and utterly tempted. If I weren't any smarter, I'd think Aphrodite was this man. "I don't want you to regret anything."

"I could never regret you."

But he's hit a heartstring and my confidence is dwindling. I have been known to regret—even if the only thing making me regret is grief.

"I know this is complicated with me," I say. My voice is hoarse. "But I need you to kiss me, Jordan."

He presses a delicate kiss to the top of my head, his hands on the nape of my neck pulling me forward.

I release a coarse laugh. "That is not the kind of kiss I meant."

"What kind of kiss did you mean?" Jordan asks, his eyes killer and vicious.

"You know the kind I mean."

He presses another kiss to my forehead. "Like this?"

I am growing antsy and impatient. "No. Try again."

"Why don't you just show me?" He laughs a little, a smile growing on his tender lips.

If I could just reach out and touch them...

I do. I run my thumb over his full, pink lips, stained a minuscule amount of orange by our drinks. *I really, really want to climb inside this man and make my home here. Why don't I show him?*

I put a gentle kiss on his lips, much gentler than my body yearns for. A kiss that says, *You are worth the wait.* He takes a shuddering breath, and I can tell he too is growing impatient by the way both of his hands have slid down to my ass, bracing me tightly, closely against him.

"Is that what you meant, Ro?" Jordan asks me, his hands cupping my butt, his arms straining, desperate to pick me up.

His voice echoes in my head. *He doesn't want me to regret it. Let's go slow.*

"It's what I meant."

He finally lifts me in the air, and I wrap my legs around him. I get a whiff of his cologne, and I am immediately an addict. He smells like citrus neroli and fresh ginger. He places me onto my sofa, and stares at me for what seems like an eternity before leaning down over me and slowly pressing his lips into mine.

His kiss lasts only a few seconds, but it feels like another miniature eternity before he slides his tongue over mine, giving me a taste of blood orange and his breath. The butterflies in my tummy take over and before I can reach up and grab his face to pull him into me, he's broken away and taken a step back.

"I think I should go home," he says, hurriedly turning around.

"What? Why?" I'm startled back into real life, out of the daydream I was in.

"It's getting late," Jordan says, still not turning around, searching for his long-forgotten sunglasses.

"So what?" I ask, craving another hit from his touch. I *am* an addict. The words come tumbling out of my mouth before I can stop them yet again. "Just stay here."

That gets him to turn around. And my eyes are immediately drawn to what he clearly didn't want me to see. The front of his pants bulges spectacularly out of shape and I am enthralled. The monster inside of me, totally pleased, saying, *this is exactly what I wanted.* But it's clear that this isn't what Jordan wanted.

I want him to stay and shed his clothes. Give me all he's got.

"You don't have to stay," I gulp.

"I'll call you before you go to bed."

Who is the one who wants to go slow? Me or him?

It's decidedly him when he's rushing out the door, and I am left on my couch alone.

Chapter 15

It's my turn to go after him. *That's what this is.* Part of me wants to rampage, to tornado all over the room. *How could he leave right now? What kind of asshole does that?*

Part of me wants to comfort him. *It's okay, I don't bite.*

I haul myself up and off the sofa, and bolt for the door. It's only been a minute. *He could still be out there.* There is no need to unlatch the lock, so I just swing the door open into the apartment, and sure enough, there he is. Pacing the hall like he's just gotten fired.

Petunia wheezes at my feet.

"Are you going to come back in?" I call to Jordan, like he called out to me. "I won't ask twice."

He paces over my way, rubbing his hands over his face. "I'm sorry, Ro."

"You're allowed to be nervous, too," I tell him, crossing my arms in the doorway in an attempt to seem in control when in reality all I wanted to do was hold his giant frame in my arms. "But don't rush out the door next time."

Thank god, he has the sense to stick around.

"It's been a long time since I've been in a relationship, too, you know," Jordan announces, like he's broadcasting a documentary or doing a *60 Minutes* segment.

"Then we're in the same boat together. It's obviously been a long time for me too." I uncross my arms, and cross them again over my chest, feeling especially vulnerable talking about my lack of relationship history. "If it helps, we don't have to label it."

Jordan takes a pause the size of Alpha Centauri. I am begging him to say anything, something next. But he doesn't.

Finally he says, "I want to label it, though."

"What do you want to label it?"

"I don't know. I don't know the word for it." *Of course he doesn't.* "I just know I don't want you in someone else's apartment or in someone else's arms."

He pulls me into the hallway, into his arms. I am squashed flush against his chest. My cheek pressed to a chiseled pectoral muscle. *I could die here, and I'd be happy.*

"I think I can manage that." His shirt muffles my response. "And you won't go anywhere else, either?"

"I can manage that."

"I think that's called being exclusive, Jordan."

"Then we'll be exclusive." He laughs into my hair. "Smart ass."

"It's not being a smart ass if I'm right, and you just couldn't think of the word."

"Being a smart ass is about inflection, Rosemary. Not intention."

I huff a big sigh as if I were Petunia. "Would you like to come inside now?"

He picks me up by my waist and carries me two steps over the threshold of my apartment before setting me down. I take his hand and walk him over to my sofa where we sit, my legs draped over his, and I'm in the crook of his arm and lap.

"Rosemary." Jordan says my name the way one would say *I love you, darling.* Every time he says it, I emerge a little further from the cracks he's breaking in my shell.

"Hmm?" My lips mere inches from his, silently begging him to shut up and kiss me.

"How long is your lease here?"

What? Why would he ask that? Now of all times?

"It's month to month," I answer, snapping out of my sultry daydreams. "They wouldn't give me a year-long lease. Why do you ask?"

Jordan cranes his neck to look around my living space. "I think we should try to find you a better apartment somewhere. This place is cramped and falling apart. A place where you can have a real painting studio."

He looks in the direction of the corner of my living room that now houses all of my painting supplies. Basically the entire southern corner is now a makeshift studio, with two easels, a stack of canvases and varying sizes of cans, jars and containers of paint.

And he's not wrong.

I survey the space. This apartment *is* cramped and falling apart. While Gio had helped design the apartments in this building, some of them had their budgets slashed and therefore corners were cut. This is one of them.

My vinyl countertops peeled, and the laminate floors dented easily. The walls had strange little bubbles from being painted over any number of times—the landlord special—as Gio had called it. The sofa and my painting studio take up the majority of the living room with the coffee table bumping my media console with the television.

"If you think this is cramped, you should see my bedroom," I laugh. My bed is against the wall. "Junior, one-bed that could fit a king? My ass."

Jordan looks at me sternly. "You have such a potty mouth, you know that, right?"

"It's from my mother." I smile smugly. *It is.*

"Still. I think we should try to find you a better place. Your budget isn't that bad. Why'd you even want to stay in this building after everything that happened?"

I look at Jordan thoughtfully, my brow knit, and I reach to rub my temple. That's a difficult question to answer, and I'm sure I know the answer myself.

"It was a comfort, I think. To know Gio was in the walls somewhere." I pause for a moment. "Why're you always trying to fix my life? First a date, now an apartment?" I'm only a little peeved. *It's nice that he cares so much.*

"You're just so helpless." Jordan looks at me, studying the wrinkles that have formed in my forehead. "Helpless in the best way. I just want to make sure you're safe."

"I'm helpless in the worst way," I decide. "Do you want some tea?"

"I'm always up for tea."

I leap off the sofa and bound the four steps it takes to get to the conjoined kitchen to turn the kettle on. I am a self-proclaimed tea snob and while I love boiling water over the gas burner, sometimes the convenience of an electric kettle beats out the old-school style.

"Let me ask *you* a question now," I demand playfully, getting two mugs from the cabinet above the sink.

"Anything."

"Why'd you name your restaurant The Red Kettle?" I pour steaming hot water into cups with Petunia's face on them.

"Growing up, one of the only things my umma brought back from Korea was a small red kettle. It always sat on the actual highest shelf in our kitchen, and she'd never let us touch it." Jordan holds out a hand to indicate about how high the shelf was. "One day, my youngest sister, you know her, climbed up there and shattered it trying to take it down. My mother was devastated."

Jordan gets up off the sofa now, too, and stands across the kitchen island staring at me while he finishes his story. "Of course, Mae was only eight or nine years old. It was hard for her to understand. But it stuck with me. So I named the restaurant after my mother's kettle. So, she'd always have, it in a way."

"That's really sweet, actually." I hold the teeming cup of tea in front of my face, breathing in the hot fumes of orange pekoe. "When are you moving your umma in with you?"

"I don't know, actually." Jordan looks down at his own mug. "The renovations are going to be quite over what I budgeted. And…" He trails off for a moment, and he lets go of his mug.

"After all you told me about Gio, I felt wrong about renovating the apartment. It really is beautiful as it is. I'm not the one who should be breaking down walls."

He takes a hefty pause in which I say nothing.

This surely can only mean one thing.

I take a small sip of tea.

"I'll be selling the apartment once I find a new place."

There it is.

"Where will you go?"

"Somewhere in the Village." Jordan looks at me reassuringly, his lips pressed into the tiniest inkling of a smile, the tiniest bit of twinkle in his eyes. "Somewhere not too far from you."

"I wasn't worried." *Yes, I was.*

"It's too much having you so close." Jordan's eyes crinkle as he laughs. They make him look so much more tempting than he is without the wrinkles.

"Being enticed is the least of my worries."

"It's one of mine." Jordan hides his smile behind his mug.

The thought suddenly pops into my mind: I should give him a house key. In case of emergencies. And Petunia. I open the newly decided upon junk drawer in my kitchen and dig around for my extra set of keys.

"I have something for you, and I promise not to throw them at you."

"What are you talking about?"

I close the drawer and set a pair of keys onto the counter in front of him.

"My apartment keys. In case of emergencies."

"In case of emergencies," Jordan repeats, like it's a question. "What kind of emergency would you be having that I need to let myself in without you?"

"I don't know. Maybe I fell in the shower or something." I *pft* a sigh and add, "Just take them! It would make me feel better if someone had them."

"If you say so."

"In case I lock myself out. There." I'm pleased to have a real reason.

"I'll make you an extra set. I had the locks changed." Jordan jingles the keys at me. "I have to get going for real this time, Ro. I'm sorry. I told Murphy I'd meet him at eight for drinks."

It's 7:30. Time has flown like a plane in the jet stream.

"To talk shit about your date?" I'm sarcastic as hell.

"Of course not." Jordan places his mug in my sink without me even asking. *What manners.* "I'll call you before bed, okay?"

"Okay."

Jordan presses a gentle kiss on the top of my head and closes the door gently behind him—and I am alone for the second time in one night.

***

So much of my life is spent waiting. Waiting for Gio to come home. Waiting for group therapy. Waiting for a new commission to come in. Waiting for tomorrow, waiting for the day after tomorrow.

And now, I spend my entire night waiting for my phone call. I am obsessed with my phone. I check after my shower. *No missed calls.* An episode of a house flipping show. *No missed calls.* Petunia's walk. *No missed calls. No missed calls. No missed calls.*

I'm clear on what we agreed upon re: exclusivity, but I still have a thousand unanswered questions and I don't even know what will come barrelling out of my mouth the second I open it to answer the phone as soon as he calls. I am beyond flustered.

He's making me feel all kinds of things I haven't felt in years and all I really want to do is shove them in a used gym duffel bag and drop it off in the closest park.

I'm exclusive with a man I met three weeks ago, who up until a week ago, I thought didn't like me. I want to laugh hysterically, but all that comes up is a strained sigh because as much as I'm overwhelmed, I'm happy with this arrangement.

This is what I wanted, isn't it? Someone to love. Someone to hold.

And I have it. So why does it feel so wrong still?

Why does it feel like a betrayal of a dead man?

I plan my next move. Is it better to obsess over the past or the future?

Should I open the can of worms that is crying over Gio's photo, clothes and things that I've preserved over the years? Do I need to grieve one last time before I go into the future that is coming faster than I anticipated?

I picture myself in a familiar scenario I've been in many times before: I'm on my bedroom floor, an Arcade Fire vinyl playing over the stereo. I'm clutching the last shirt he wore, with a thousand photos strewn over the floor, surrounding me like a sea of memories. I'm startled by this daydream when I realize it's at the old apartment. I have yet to grieve in this new place. What a shame, I can't wait to christen it with my tears. Maybe I ought to overthink the future instead.

I daydream about what my relationship with Jordan could look like. It could really go one of two ways—just fine or really, really badly. We could get along really well. We could be happy. I could see us being together for a long, long time.

And as soon as I'm picturing Jordan proposing to me on top of a rooftop overlooking the city, I'm hit with a frightening thought, and I am bent and mangled like a T-boned car.

What if Jordan dies, too?

What would I do?

I don't think I could handle it again. I know I couldn't handle it again.

I don't even know what to make of the thought. I couldn't picture myself losing two lovers. No one pictures themselves losing one. *What would I do if Jordan died?* My chest tightens at the thought of him not being here anymore. Not calling me every night. Not kissing me. Not feeding me food at his restaurant.

What if he's dead and that's why he's not calling me?

I picture him in a thousand different scenarios, all with the same ending: Jordan lying cold and dead at a morgue. Being transferred into a wooden coffin. Being lowered into the ground. Me, bursting into uncontrollable tears at just the mention of his name. *Just like Gio.*

I shake my head and clear the thought. Thinking about the future is supposed to be happy. It's not productive to think this way. I think back to group therapy. Imagining the pain of losing someone only amplifies it when you have to do it for real. But still, I hold my head in my hands, tears brimming on my short, stubby lashes.

Please don't die, Jordan. Let me die first.

My phone finally rings.

INCOMING CALL: JORDAN PARK.

I press the green answer button.

"Hellooo, Rosemary!" Jordan's voice is a little slurred and slow.

I feel the warmth of relief spread through my chest. *He's not dead. Of course he's not, you weirdo.* "I'm so glad you called."

"Of course. I told you I'd call." Jordan's voice is an immediate comfort, even though I'd seen him only a few short hours ago. *Anxiety will do that to a bitch, won't it.*

"How was drinks with Murphy?" I ask, a feeble attempt to make conversation.

"It was good to see him. I've been so busy with the restaurant. And you." I can hear his smile through the phone.

"I missed you." I tell him, my voice is honest and hardhearted.

"I missed you too, Ro." I feel my heart lift and brighten the more he speaks. *He's alive and just fine.* "What's going on?"

"What do you mean?" I ask. Tears are visible in my voice.

"You've never told me you missed me before. You sound like you're about to cry."

I press myself to try to not cry. "I'm not crying," I deny. "I just…" I trail off for a moment. I don't want to scare him off with my crazy worries over this. "Just promise me you won't die, Jordan." I say his name like a command.

"I won't die, Rosemary." Jordan's voice is a loving caress of my face through the phone. "I promise."

"Thank you." I inhale a great, big breath like I'm about to do a yoga pose. "I was just concerned that maybe something happened to you."

"I promise nothing will happen to me. Don't cry, Ro," Jordan reassures me.

"You can't die on me." Tears stream relatively silently down my face. *I cry so damn much in front of this man.* "I'm not crying."

"I won't die on you. I can hear you crying, you know." Jordan laughs lightly, but not at me. "Do you want me to come downstairs?"

"You would?" *I didn't even think to ask.*

"Of course I would."

Without me saying anything else, the phone hangs up. Within three minutes, I hear the lock click open, and the door gently closing. My house is whisper quiet, and I can hear him take off his shoes and align them in the doorway. He makes his way through my barebones kitchen and I hear him gently press my bedroom door open.

The only lights are a buzzing set of old string lights with several burnt-out bulbs draped across my window. I am in a tangled mess of bed covers and sheets, sitting up against my bed frame, my hair lazily tied up, a trail of tissues from my nightstand to my bedroom floor.

Jordan stands in the doorway, wearing a crisp olive green linen shirt and black pants, looks dressed to kill. His black hair is combed half across his forehead and half to the side, and he looks like he could be straight out of any popular Korean drama.

It takes everything in me not to get up and put my arms around him like some kind of leech even though I am a boogery mess.

"Welcome to my home," I say flatly, unsure of what to do. I suck up an ugly, disgusting sniffle.

"What happened to you?" Jordan laughs painlessly and effortlessly. "I was only gone a few hours." He walks to sit on the edge of my bed, patting Petunia on his way.

"Anxiety got the better of me."

"Happens to the best of us." He puts his hands on his knees and looks at me sideways.

"I don't know what came over me." *Actually, I do know what came over me. I was afraid he'd get sick and die. Why can't I just tell him that?*

I really don't want to scare him off.

"I don't want to scare you away."

"Rosemary. Look at me."

I do as I am told and look up at him sincerely.

"You have cried in front of me several times now. Nothing you will ever do will scare me away."

"You mean that?"

Jordan pulls a tissue out of the box and uses it to wipe under my nose.

What a true gentleman.

"I mean it. Would I be wiping your nose if I didn't?"

"Some people do fucked up things, Jordan." I laugh through whatever straggling tears I have left.

"This is not one of my fucked up things." Jordan scooches closer to me, carefully making sure his feet do not touch the bed, and that I remain balled up against the wall, and takes my face in his hands. This time I feel more like a delicate piece of stained glass than a soccer ball. "Don't act like you're a fucked up thing. You've been through a lot."

He's right. I have been treating myself like a fucked up thing. And I have been through a lot.

184

"You are not the things you carry." Jordan wipes my eyes for me.

I am not what I have been.

"Can I kiss you?" I ask him.

He answers by pressing a tender, unguarded kiss to my lips. This kiss is all sweetness, all safety, no lust, no infatuation. I take his face in my hands, and they find their way to the back of his head, through his soft, luscious hair.

I find sanctuary and shelter in him as he kisses me, and I pull him closer to bring him next to me. He breaks our kiss and I miss the heat of his lips immediately, but am guarded by the heat of his body being so close to mine. He puts a hand through my hair, and while he gets caught in the tangles of my curls, it doesn't stop him from grabbing handful after handful.

I suddenly feel too vulnerable, too naked, even though I'm decked out in the most ridiculous pajamas I own. Our lips are dangerously close to touching again, and I know if they do, I won't be able to stop there. *I want him to stay here with me.*

"Wait," I interject the moment he leans back towards me.

"Yeah?" Jordan stops in his tracks, but his eyes remain closed.

"Will you spend the night with me?" I ask, my voice filled with genuine need. "Not like to sleep with me, I mean, to have sex." I stumble and teeter over my words. "Just to sleep in my bed. Together."

Jordan breaks out into his winning grin. "Of course I'll stay with you. We don't have to do anything you don't want to do."

"The same goes for you."

"What time do you normally go to sleep? You don't happen to have some shorts I could borrow, do you? Or do you mind if I sleep with no pants?" Jordan asks me a bunch of rapid-fire questions and I have no clear answers to any of them.

He crawls away from me and off the bed and begins unbuttoning his shirt to reveal a white muscle tank underneath. It clings to his smooth skin like plastic wrap, and it takes everything in me not to let my jaw drop. He is utterly delicious. *This is all mine, now.*

"I…" I don't have a single answer. "You…" The more buttons he undoes, the fewer words I have to say. And when he slips the shirt off entirely and his forearms are bare, I just want to throw myself at him until he accepts.

He is so perfectly perfect. Jordan has a hell of a body. Triceps, biceps, you name it, he's got it. *This isn't even the first time I'm seeing him.* I think back to the first time I saw him like this. *In that stupidly tiny towel.* I imagine it as my towel.

"Hello? Earth to Rosemary?" Jordan laughs as he folds his shirt and places it on my wardrobe.

"I don't have any shorts you can borrow," I say quickly to make up for my silence.

"Should I leave and come back?"

"Don't leave!" I say before my better judgment kicks in. *Fuck. You idiot!*

"Sure thing, Ro." He walks down along the edge of my bed again and undoes his belt buckle. With each passing second, my heart beats faster and faster. *Here it comes.*

I try to mentally prepare myself for what I know I'm about to see, but still, I can't manage to be anything but stunned when he unzips his pants to take them off. I force myself not to wince. *Why am I the one embarrassed? He's the one taking his pants off!*

So, he's a briefs guy.

"What's the matter with you?" Jordan asks while folding his pants to stack on top of his shirt. He turns around to set his phone on top of his neatly folded pile.

"You have a great ass," I tell him earnestly. He does.

His black underpants stretch like nobody's business.

"I like that you have no filter."

When he turns around, my eyes almost roll back into my head. *I'm fucked, I'm fucked.* He clearly has the package to match the ass, and I swallow the growing lump in my throat. The glimpse I got earlier did not prepare me for this. *I'm not ready.* I try to convince myself I am.

"Where do you want me, Ro?" Jordan asks me dutifully.

"Just...here...I guess." I gesture broadly to my bed. It's pressed up against the wall by the window to make more space by the doorway for my wardrobe and Petunia's bed. I'm huddled in the corner, bathrobe and Snoopy pajamas on.

His skin looks caramel colored in this light and when he lies down next to me, I feel like I'm melting in it. Once I lie down, Jordan turns so we are face to face.

"When do you want to go to sleep?" he asks, his voice husky and low.

"I don't have a set time." I look at his dark brown eyes, and I find a million safety nets within them. *This is exactly what I need.* "But I am ready whenever you are."

"Can I put my arm around you?" He acts like a reverse big spoon by placing a hesitant arm around me. "I don't want to go too fast for you, Rosie."

The way he says Rosie makes my heart burst.

"This is just fine with me." I tell him, and my eyes are sleepy as he draws me near and close to his chest.

"I feel safe with you." It's true.

"I'm glad you do."

Jordan presses an apprehensive but soft kiss to my forehead

before closing his eyes.

"Goodnight Rosemary."

Jordan keeps his eyes closed and doesn't say anything for what feels like an infinite amount of time, so before long, I also close my eyes.

"Goodnight Jordan."

Chapter 16

When I wake, there's a dip in the mattress where Jordan used to be. It's early morning, not earlier than seven o'clock. Panic rises in my chest when I don't see him. My eyes dart around the room, and I find him. He's there, standing in the corner of my bedroom, pulling on his shirt and pants.

"Where are you going?" My voice is a rustle of leaves in the wind.

"To take a shower and get some clothes. I'll be back." He walks towards me, his undershirt gone and his linen shirt unbuttoned exposing his supple, malleable skin.

"When?" I admire his tattoos. I want to trace them all. I want to paint them all.

Jordan lets out a loose and airy chuckle. "I don't know, Ro, twenty minutes?"

"I'm timing you."

He curls his arms around me and delicately kisses my lips. *Morning breath, who? Even his morning breath is utterly sexy.*

"I'll be back in nineteen, then."

I should have let him use my shower.

As soon as he's out the door, I wiggle free from my covers and inspect myself in the mirror. *I should take a shower too.* I undress one by one, imagining Jordan taking my clothes off of me. The thought sends a shiver up and down my spine. I can't believe I slept in my bathrobe. The last time I did that I was sick with the flu.

I turn the hot water on, and Petunia whines at my feet.

"I'll be quick. Promise." She plops down on my bathroom rug in response.

I rinse out my mangled curls and detangle them with my fingers. I quickly but thoroughly scrub the important parts of my body before dousing myself in cold water. Petunia's anxious cries become more and more persistent.

"Okay, okay!" I tell her. I turn the water off and slip back into my bathrobe. Normally, I hate taking her out while commando like this, but she's running out of time, and I'll be damned if she has an accident in this house.

I do my hair quickly up into a plopped towel and toe on a pair of sneakers, and instead of leashing her, I just pick Petunia up and after locking the door, quickly run down the stairs with her in my arms. I reach the grass out front, and I promptly plop her down to do her business.

She makes a point to sniff around for an extra-long time. *That cheeky dog.*

As soon as she's finished, I pick her up and march back inside. When I unlock the front door, I'm surprised to see that Jordan is already waiting for me at my kitchen island, dressed in his chef's whites.

"Where were you?" he asks swiftly.

"I took Petunia out."

"Only in your robe?"

"What are you talking about?" *Does he know?* Petunia wiggles out of my arms and greets Jordan like he's just another friendly face, and not the man intent on getting on my nerves at 7:30 in the fucking morning.

The chiding grin on his face says he *certainly knows.*

"Are you naked under there, Rosemary?"

I freeze up and hearing him say the word *naked* makes me blush harder than I ever thought I could.

"It's none of your business if I am or not."

"It is my business if my girlfriend is going outside in only her bathrobe."

"I'm not your girlfriend," I correct him, and even though he stands with his arms open, I deny him the chance to hold me. "And I *am* wearing clothes."

I am definitely not wearing clothes.

"Prove it. Take it off."

I get ready to undo the belt of my robe, a fiendish grin sprawling on my face, but before I can give him an eyeful, I bolt into my bedroom to put on real clothes.

I hear him call out that one day I will be his girlfriend. *One day. Not today.*

I dress quickly in my painting coveralls. I tie up my hair and do my makeup in my small bedroom mirror. It isn't like me to wear makeup often, but I want to impress the man sitting in my kitchen. I so badly want to be the rosy-cheeked girl he claims to be seeing.

It's Monday, and our usual routine is certainly shattered from last night. Instead of meeting him in the lobby, I meet him in my living room. Today will be the day I finish the mural, a week ahead of schedule. I don't ask him about payment.

We walk hand in hand out of the building, like a real couple would, and stop at Sheila's for pastries and tea. We walk to the restaurant this morning instead of taking the subway and by the time we get there it's almost nine o'clock.

I contemplate messing up the mural just to drag it out longer to spend more time with him. As Jordan unlocks the door and steps inside, he pauses to take in the mural.

There is really not much left to do. Add some finishing touches to the couple standing on the shore of the lake, and perhaps to the trees and mountains in the background. A week to dry to be safe, and it'll be ready to have patrons sitting in front of it.

Jordan asks the question I've been sitting on the answer to.

"When will you be finished?" he asks.

"Today," I tell him, honestly. "I don't think I'll need the last week."

Three weeks ago, I was looking forward to this day, but now I dread it. No more walking to the restaurant with Jordan in the morning. No more chatting the day away while doing something I love. I'm not sure if I'll be able to see him every day again. There is no way he can stay over at my place every single night.

"It looks beautiful, Rosemary," he tells me earnestly.

"Of course it does," I laugh. "I wouldn't paint you a shitty painting."

"What will you do now?"

"I'm not sure. Look for another commission, I guess." Normally, when I'm on top of my game, I have another lined up as one finishes, but I've been so distracted with my budding romance that I've totally forgotten. I fidget in front of the mural, holding my paint brush box, unsure where to start or what to say to Jordan. We stand side-by-side to look at the work.

"I have a proposal for you." Jordan sticks his hand out like he's writing a checklist in the air. "Help my mother paint again."

"Your mother?"

"Yes. She clearly misses it." Jordan's eyes are big and full of hope. "Paint with her every day for the next week and I'll pay you an additional thousand. And if you get along, you can keep doing it."

"You have a deal." I don't even hesitate to answer. *Rent is coming up after all.* "You don't feel weird about paying me?"

"Why would I? My feelings for you are totally separate from our professional relationship. You are an excellent painter, Rosemary."

"I'm pleased to hear that." I smile at him. "Can I kiss you?"

"Why couldn't you?" Jordan turns towards me, his hands moving to my elbows, moving my arms around his waist.

"We're at your restaurant. Someone might see!" Despite my reservations, my hands flatten against the small of his back, eager to get their fill of his body before I have to start painting.

"I haven't been keeping you a secret." Jordan's voice changes to a serious tone I've only heard him use once or twice. "Murphy already knows."

"Did you tell him last night?" I ask.

"No."

"What do you mean?"

"He knew the moment I met you."

"What?"

"He called it first, in fact."

"Of course he did." I don't even know what to say.

"I knew I wanted you the moment I laid eyes on you." Jordan confirms my suspicions. *He didn't just buy me tea or help me for no reason. He* did *swipe on me on purpose.* I know that he likes me, but it feels nice to have been right about it all along.

"You're a better person than I am." I turn to hide my face and the devilish laugh I can't help but release. "I only started liking you after I saw your Tinder profile photos."

"I forgive you, Rosemary," Jordan teases.

"You're easy on the eyes, what can I say?" I have no chance at defending myself. I look back at him with a smile plastered to my face. *Is this what being happy is like? I finally have someone to give all my love to.*

"Do you want to know a secret?" Jordan whispers in my ear, his voice suddenly sultry and authentic, the teasing totally gone.

"Absolutely I do."

"I didn't know you were actually naked under your bathrobe. It was just a lucky guess." I can hear his smile pressed up against my ear.

"You little *shit*."

"Hey, hey, be nice now." He presses a kiss to my earlobe.

"I'm always nice." I turn my cheek to his lips, and he kisses it straight away. His lips are like hot fire and ash on my cool skin.

I bring my arms up to his neck, and I'm almost standing on his toes, but I reach up and brush my lips against his. *It's fucking delicious.* He tastes like fresh lemon, a fresh start, and like everything I'd been missing the last three years. I can't get enough.

We probably look like two horny teenagers making out in the restaurant, but I feel rejuvenated. He's awakened something in me I didn't know I had left. He wraps his hands around the curve of my ass and picks me up to set me on the table in front of the mural. Jordan leans forward over me, sliding his tongue over mine in a way that says *you're wanted; you're home; you're safe.*

I am terrified by what this kiss means to me, but I can't help but mirror his strength and return his desire back equally, if not fiercer. *He's the opposite of Gio in every way, but I can't help but need him.* My mind snaps. *Don't compare him to Gio. He's amazing in his own right.*

He towers over me. His hands rest on my thighs, the table now bearing the brunt of my weight, while his tongue does things to me that make me want to unravel completely.

Before I can let my anxiety stop me, I start fumbling with the buttons on his chef's jacket. His hands are caressing my sides in a way that makes me want to be naked. *How did we sleep next to each other and not do this last night?*

He's unzipping the front of my coveralls, and I'm desperate to get hands on skin whether it's his on mine, or mine on his. *Are we going to do this in a restaurant?*

I hear the bells on the front of the restaurant door jingle lightly.

I'm the one who jumps.

Busted. We are not going to do this in a restaurant.

"Christ, you two." I can hear the eye roll in Murphy's voice. "I'll be damned, the one day I come to work early, I catch my boss acting like he's in a porno."

Jordan's lips are bright pink and swollen from my hungry kisses, his hair mildly tousled, his collar lopsided, and I bet I look worse than him.

"What kind of softcore porn are you watching?" Jordan fires back, doing up the four buttons I managed to undo. All I can manage to do is blink and try to retie my hair. Murphy makes his way back to the kitchen, not even bothering to answer Jordan.

"I have work to do, darling." Jordan kisses the top of my head. I'm still sitting on the table mildly stunned. "But I'll check on you in a bit." Before I can say anything, he too disappears into the kitchen.

I press the back of my hand to my lips, as if I can't believe I just did that.

I really can't believe I just did that.

Jordan brings out something totally different in me that I never saw when I was with Gio. *Has this part of me been here the whole time?* I don't know. *I guess dry humping in a restaurant gets a girl to reflect.*

Even though she's a nameless, unidentified figure, I add flecks of red to the woman's hair and flecks of golden yellow to the man's eyes.

It isn't until I'm painting the curls of her hair, and the curve of a tattoo that I realize I'm painting Jordan and me. *I've been painting us this whole time.* Us sitting on the banks of the East River. But instead of New York City as the backdrop, it's an unknown mountain range. Somewhere else is the only place I imagine really being with Jordan. New York City had always been Gio's. *But maybe it could belong to both of them.* It had to. *I am in love with him. With who?* I ask myself. *With who?* I picture them side by side.

Jordan gets old and wrinkled. Gio stays twenty-three. Jordan holds me and caresses me. Gio is in pixels on a screen. Jordan is a real boy who moves and talks and is animated. Gio is an old home movie, a memory that skips and has repeated tics. Jordan is undeniably bright, and bursting at the seams with love and devotion. Gio is a rock in a pile of dirt, perpetually six feet of distance between us. *You can't be in love with a dead man.*

In the past, I would have said: *If I love anything as much as I love you, let my head be cleaved from my neck.*

But now, there's Jordan. He's here. He's alive. He's warm and impassioned and ardent. I'd keep him and throw myself away for him. He would do the same for me.

I love him.

I would be beside myself if I couldn't have him.

I have to tell him. And I will. But not yet. I have barely just admitted it to myself. I want to be sure. *Is a month of knowing someone too soon to tell? Have I just latched on to the first person who gave me the time of day?*

I know that isn't true. Jordan and I are not so different after all. If he was jam, I was preserves. Stalactite and stalagmite. Cardamom and cinnamon. Rosemary and thyme. Rosemary and her man. I love him for him, not because of his convenience.

I love him.

Not loved, but love.

I make sure to paint a dragon tattoo on the man.

Later that afternoon, after Jordan walks me to my front door, leaving Murphy to handle the lunch service, only smelling a little like fish, he hands me a crisp white envelope.

"What's this?"

"Open it and look."

It's a check for $8,600. This had to be the payment for the rest of the mural, but it was too much.

"What is this?" I repeat. "This is like $3,000 too much," I tell him. "I haven't started painting with your umma yet. Speaking of that...Jordan, this is too much, really."

"Pay your rent, Ro."

"What?"

"I said, pay your rent, Ro." Jordan crosses his arms. "Until you find a better place."

"I can't take this, Jordan."

"My restaurant is doing well, Rosemary. We sold some of my mother's paintings. Just take it, please. I want to help you."

I feel tears well in my eyes. *I'm a crier. What can I say?*

"I can't take this," I tell him again.

"Rosemary, if you don't take it, I'll go to the landlord and pay your rent myself."

"You might have to do that." I chuckle through a single tear, swearing to myself not to cry. "I'll do it. Because you asked."

"Good." Jordan wraps me into a salmon-smelling hug. "You'll meet my umma tomorrow. Same time at the restaurant, okay? Just for a few hours so my sister can have some time off."

"That's fine with me. I've been thinking about planning some activities for her. I'll tell you about it later."

"I'll call you when I get home, okay?"

"Okay."

I send him off with a short kiss as he bounds down the hallway towards the stairs. His long legs get him there much faster than I wished. *Hate to watch you go, but love to watch you leave.*

Let the waiting game begin.

I take Petunia out for a walk. I find some familiarity in my old routines, and I run some errands. On the subway, I scour craigslist, job boards and Facebook groups for potential jobs. Nothing quite catches my eye, so I focus on creating activities to do with Jordan's mother.

After a quick google search, I settle on designing greeting cards with her. I'm sure how severe her Alzheimer's is, so it should be simple enough that she can ultimately just paint on some paper and we can take it from there. Using my new funds from Jordan, I purchase cardstock, as well as her own set of watercolors and brushes. I will bring my own from home.

It takes me a moment, but I realize how much I'm looking forward to this.

I'm nervous to meet his umma, but I'm trying to think of her just as a client for painting lessons. *Painting lessons.* I open my Facebook app, and I make a rare post.

Would anyone be interested in painting lessons?

I don't know what qualifies me to teach, other than my degree and my portfolio, but maybe someone out there is interested if

Jordan is. I don't want to keep taking money from him. We are a team now. I have to find steady work that doesn't come from…*my boyfriend.*

I choke on the word in my brain a little bit. I'm not quite ready for that word, but that's what Jordan is to me, isn't he?

***

When my phone rings around 10:00 p.m. I can't pick up fast enough.

"Hello?" I answer, as if I don't know who it is.

"It's me." Jordan's voice is dark and stormy.

"How was your day?"

"I missed you. That's pretty much how my day was. How was yours?"

"I planned some fun things for your umma and I to do tomorrow. I wish I could see you right now."

"Please don't tell me where you are, or I'll let myself in." Jordan's voice crackles huskily over the phone.

Sixty-five heartbeats feel like an eternity when there's silence on the line.

I hear a knock on my door. *Has he been waiting outside my door?* When I hear the click of my lock and the beep of the phone, I know it's him.

"Jordan," is all I can manage to whisper. "Just let yourself in."

Standing in my living room, I'm greeted immediately by an untamed, unrelenting kiss that I've been waiting for since this morning.

There's no turning back now.

Chapter 17

He wraps his arms around my neck, and I hang on to him like my life depends on it. He presses kisses into my cheek, my forehead, my neck, and I stand there and take it like the champ I am.

"Every second I spend without you is like eternity," Jordan whispers into a kiss behind my ear. "Where have you been all my life?"

"Waiting until you were ready for me," is my answer. My hands follow no laws as they climb up into his hair. I kiss him like a threat. *Kiss me back, or else. Kiss me back, or you won't live to regret it.* I grab his arms, his chest, his ass, anything I can get my little hands on.

"I don't think I'll ever be ready for you." Jordan pulls me to him, closer than I thought possible, his hand at the base of my spine. I leech energy from him. He fuels me. "You're too much."

"But you have to be. I'm ready." I swallow even though there's nothing in my throat. Jordan moves his hands to cup my face. I am a boiling kettle, and he is the fire from within, the burner on a stove, the campfire in the wilderness. "You don't have to be," I falter.

"I'm ready," he replies.

"You're crazy," is all I have to say to him.

"You make me crazy." His hands have moved from my cheeks to my temples to my scalp. *He makes me crazy.*

"You are taking this agonizingly slow," I remark.

"What's the rush?" Jordan's hands are fiddling at the tie of my bathrobe. "I think you're the one taking this slow."

I have no answer except to wrap a finger around an empty belt loop. He's dressed in black pants with a black button up shirt, the fishmonger smell clearly long gone. *I'm going to do this and have a shit ton to talk about at therapy tomorrow.* I yank his waist closer to mine like some kind of wildebeest.

"Why are you always in this bathrobe?" he asks.

"I live in this bathrobe. Why are you always in my apartment late at night?"

"You invited me in." Jordan's hands have moved from the tie to place a hand on each of my hips.

"You were at my door. You didn't have to come in."

"Are you always this defensive?" Jordan squeezes my hip tighter before removing his hands and holding them palm up in surrender.

We are face to face, nose to nose, eyelash to eyelash.

"Yes."

He's teasing me, and I'm endlessly frustrated with myself because I don't know if I want to smack him or screw him. My hands are shaking when I reach up to touch his face. He has a small amount of stubble, like he shaved yesterday but not this morning, and his clear eyes study my every move.

"Take your time, Rosemary. We don't have to do anything you don't want to."

We are lit by the flicker of the TV set, and I'm as sure of what I want, as sure as the tide rolls up the beach and the wind blows the grass. I spread my fingers over his cheeks, running my thumb over his lips. *I'm the one in charge here.*

Jordan knows it too. His arms are limp at his sides, waiting for my instruction and guidance, and I place them on my bathrobe ties. He unknots my bathrobe but doesn't take it off.

"Stop antagonizing me. Participate a little," I command. *Or participate a lot.*

In response, Jordan shifts the bathrobe off my left shoulder. Then my right. Then down both arms. He carries it delicately in his arms and sets it on the back of my kitchen table chair. It feels like such an intimate act, a declaration of love, because although it's only a bathrobe, it feels like he's removed whatever armor I had left.

Standing there in my T-shirt and shorts, he approaches me once more, and before I can make a break and run for it, he kisses me fiercely, and I am entranced completely. He kisses away all of my worries, all my doubts about this, and I tell him *thank you* with my kisses in return.

Jordan puts a tender hand on the back of my head and uses it to control the depth of our kiss. I hand control over to him, and I am so glad he's taken charge. *I don't think I could manage to be this smooth.* My body yearns for him, and I tell him by dipping my fingers into the waistband of his pants and feeling the smoothness of his skin. Each time the pads of my fingers interact with his skin, lightning shocks run through me.

His fingers dig into my lower back, and he buries his face in the space below my neck. Jordan's hands are hotter than the sun, and they ease their way around my body, even though it's the first time he's touched me like this.

I force myself to squash the anxiety growing in the bottom of my tummy, that this is what I want. *I'm allowed to have a good time.*

I use everything in me to stomp out any fear I have, and I lift Jordan's shirt, my hands grazing his chest eagerly.

"Let me have you. I want nothing in return."

"I'm all yours, Rosemary," he tells me.

"I'm all yours, too, Jordan."

When he lifts me up off the ground, and carries me into my bedroom, I know I've made the right choice. I think my heart is about to beat out of my chest when he sets me on the edge of the bed and puts his thumbs under my shirt to lift it. My automatic response is to put my arms up and away so he can pull it off.

When he exposes my chest, the way he says my name sends me into another spiritual plane. "Rosemary," Jordan groans, his voice gravelly. "Why aren't you wearing a bra?"

"I'm at home. I'm not going to wear one."

"You've deprived me of taking it off."

"There will be another time, Jordan."

His fingers dip and twist underneath my breasts, holding them like they fit perfectly in his hands. Which they do, I find out, when he brushes over my nipples and sends a ripple of pleasure through my body. His kisses are electric shockwaves that my heart can barely endure. *It's been so long since someone touched me like this.*

I pull him closer onto me. He gently lays me flat on my back and puts his knees on either side of my waist. Jordan drops feverish kisses onto my collarbones, my shoulders, my breasts, and I am too flattered to do anything but grasp at his back. Each of his touches sends heat straight between my thighs.

The way his faint six pack stomach curves into soft, human rolls makes me feel like I swallowed a hurricane. *He's so fucking hot. There's no way a body should look like that.*

"Jordan. You are so fucking attractive right now." I grab hungrily for the button of his pants and feebly undo it as he takes my nipple into his mouth, and the words are stolen right out of my mouth. I want to tell him how wet I am for him.

"Rosemary," he lets out a groan that is pure heaven. "How can you taste like this?"

I don't know what I taste like, and I bet I taste like expired lotion, but he clearly is into it, and that's all that matters to me. He drops lower onto me, and I feel the weight of his maleness push into me. *Oh fuck. He's so hard, I can feel him through his pants.*

"Do you know how badly I want you, Ro?" he whispers like his life depends on it. It may as well.

"Show me," I say, mustering all the courage I have.

"Can I take these off?"

He tugs on my shorts, and I groan a *yes* as he presses a kiss just under my navel. He kisses each place he pulls fabric away from. The cool air is startling as he pulls away from my body. The second my panties are off my ankles, and before I can make a comment, he sinks his mouth between my legs and I let out a feral gasp. *He knows exactly where to put his tongue.*

Jordan's finesse is impressive. I roll my hips against his mouth and it's my turn to groan his name. I feel the pressure building in me as he licks, my hands tangling in his hair, messing up whatever hairstyle he had left.

Something in me changes when he angles my hips upward, and the heat of his tongue becomes almost unbearable. I arch into his pull, and I press myself to his tongue just as much as he pulls into my press.

"Rosemary," Jordan breathes into my body.

Hearing my own name come out of his mouth, pressed against me, gives me life.

"Your pussy tastes so good." He rewards me with a pucker of his lips and I am ready to break.

"I'm…" I start but can't finish. All that comes out of me are fragments of sentences.

This is a shipwreck for me. He is the island, the water, and the boat.

I am awash in Jordan as I buck against his face, his tongue managing final strokes as I bite on my own tongue. I shake to my core and let go. I am safe. I am loved. I am home. I am fraught with a wave of something so intense I can't put a name to it because I haven't felt it in so long.

"That's the first time I've had an orgasm with a man in three years."

Jordan barks a short laugh, and he climbs his way up to my face, his lips still swollen and damp from me, and I pull him into a kiss. His erection presses into my thigh like an iron rod.

"Can I touch you?" I ask against his lips.

"You can do anything you want, Rosemary."

I yank his pants down with unbridled ferocity, and he manages to kick them off his ankles with as much grace as an elephant. He clambers back on top of me, pushing his hands to hold the sides of my breasts.

"Jeez," I wheeze.

He shushes me with a taste of his tongue.

"Jeez yourself."

I tuck my hand into one side of his black briefs to cup the curve of his ass. It's unbelievably smooth. *No man should have an ass this smooth.* I tuck in the other hand and hold him above me, although he carries most of his weight on his knees. My head is almost flat against my headboard, Jordan's knees on either side of me.

I slide my hands around to the front and take his erection in my hands. It's more than enough. *He's fucking huge.*

"Fuck me, Rosemary," Jordan breathes out quickly through his nose.

"Literally?" I ask.

"No, figuratively." His masculine voice is strained and uneven when I run my hand up and down his length. Touching him is one thing, but seeing him is another. I pull his briefs down to expose him and my eyes are so, so hungry.

"I can't stop looking at you," I tell him as I make him sit back on his heels on top of me. I run my hands up to his chest and graze his nipples lightly with my fingertips. Jordan tips his head back in response.

"Do you have a condom?" I ask him, my breath hot and heavy against his neck.

"In my pants." He climbs off me, and I immediately miss his heat. He's back in a heartbeat though and tearing the wrapper open with ease.

"Do you want to put it on?"

I gingerly take the latex in my hand and roll it on him carefully. *It's been a while since I had to do this.* Touching him is like torture when I want him inside of me.

He brings his head and body forward and comes down onto his elbows above me and I am nearly flattened in the best possible way. The tip of him presses at my entrance and I writhe under his weight.

He push, pushes into me gently, our voices collectively groaning as he does.

"If you need to stop, just tell me, Ro." Jordan's voice is harried and urgent.

"I will. Keep going."

He gives a gentle, timid thrust and I want to tell him *more.*

It's like he knew what I was thinking when he hikes my leg up with his right hand, bending my knee. He thrusts again and I quite literally see stars.

"It's been so long, Jordan," I am already out of breath. "You feel so good."

"Don't talk, Rosie, if you don't have to," he whispers into my neck, and I swivel my hips to meet his thrusts, but he's just *so heavy* I can barely move underneath his weight. I don't say a word. "You are such a good girl."

As our bodies blend together, the lines between me and him are the same. Jordan hits a point in me that I never felt before and when he hits it over and over I can't help but unravel like a ball of string down a hill.

"Jordan," I am gasping for air against all I can stand. "I don't think I can come twice."

"Yes, you can," he commands me, and I am a willing participant. *I can.*

He thrusts boldly and I start to feel his body quake atop me. I reach my arms around his back, digging my fingernails into his skin.

"Oh, Ro." His voice is fragile and little in his big body. He gives one more heave and I feel him shake inside me and out. He puts a hot and heavy-handed kiss to my chin, missing my lips. His apology comes out breathless and as he lifts off of me, I tell him there's nothing to apologize for.

"You are something else, Jordan."

"So are you."

He stands, completely naked before me, taking off the condom. As he turns around to throw it out in the bathroom, I can't help but stare at his ass as he goes. *So fine.*

"Let me go change." He plops a wet kiss to my forehead.

"You brought clothes?" I ask him, laying naked in my own bed.

"I did. They're in the entry." He gives me a grin, and I am in over my head.

Jordan and I dress and sit side by side on my bed. He tousles my hair playfully and kisses my cheek.

"I can't believe we just did that," I tell him. My voice is more serious than I'm feeling.

"I would have done that to you the day we met if you'd let me."

"Oh, please." I turn my body to face him again. "I was such an asshole that day."

"It made me like you even more," he tells me. "The couch really wasn't a problem."

"You acted like it was the end of the world."

"I just wanted to see you again."

"You can see me every day now," I tell him, laying down to put my head in his lap.

"For that, I am so grateful," is the last thing I remember him saying before falling asleep.

***

When I wake up, I am exhausted again already. Jordan is a generous lover, and he proved it to me over and over last night. He's cradled in the crook of my arm, his eyes sleepy and still drooping heavily despite the light streaming through my open curtain.

I look at Jordan's sleeping face. He looks so peaceful and almost baby-like with his eyes closed, biting down on his lip. I want to coo and cradle him like a baby. It's almost seven o'clock and I pray that Petunia can forgive me. Jordan barely stirs when I move my arm out from underneath him.

I walk Petunia to her favorite spot around the corner of the building and make her a scrambled egg for breakfast. When I return, dolled up in my pink bathrobe, Jordan is fully awake, and his arms are outstretched, waiting for me as I open the door.

Pleased to have altered my morning routine, he beckons me into his arms.

"How'd you sleep, sleepyhead?" I ask.

"That bathrobe again," is his answer.

"It's my comfort robe," I inform him. "Do you want to eat breakfast here?"

"Are you cooking?"

"That was the plan."

"I'll cook for you, Ro." Jordan sits up, moderately bedraggled. His shirt and pants are now draped over the end of my bed frame after some late-night *activity*. He pulls his arms through his shirt but skips putting his pants back on and follows me into the kitchen, Petunia on his heels.

I pray he doesn't drip oil on himself as he cracks open three eggs into a frying pan. *That ass is a fire hazard.*

"Maybe you should leave some clothes here," I say absentmindedly.

"Yeah? That's okay with you?" Jordan asks, as if I weren't the one who suggested it.

"Of course," I tell him. "I'm planning on having you spend the night again. It only makes sense."

"You don't mind me spending the night?"

"I love you spending the night." The words slipped right out of my mouth, implying that I love him. Is it too soon?

"I love spending the night here, too, Ro." He sets a perfectly fried egg on a plate in front of me, before opening my fridge, presumably to look for something to go with it.

"Why's all you got in here…" He holds up my options. "Some moldy blackberries and ketchup?"

"I haven't been to the grocery store lately."

"Promise me we'll go this afternoon," Jordan says. "In between my shifts."

"I can't. I have group therapy this afternoon." I think it's the first time I've told him.

"Group therapy for what?" His voice sounds concerned, not upset.

"Grief."

"Oh." He sets the frying pan down. "Is it really that bad?"

"No. But I like to go. It helps for when it does get bad."

"I'm glad it helps, Ro."

"You don't mind if I go?"

"Of course not. Go if it makes you feel better."

"You're sure?" *He doesn't sound too sure.*

"I'm sure." He nods, decidedly so. "We'll go grocery shopping after the dinner service."

"That would be really nice." I shovel eggs into my mouth like I'm starving. Because I am starving. "Thank you for the money, by the way. You didn't have to do that. I'll make it up to you."

"You've already made it up to me." He winks and places the frying pan in the sink, two eggs on his own plate.

"You make it sound like I'm a hooker."

"Come on, we both know you're not. Don't take me so seriously, Ro."

Jordan takes a bite of his own breakfast. The smile on his face is clear. It's perfection. As perfect as eggs can get anyway. There's something so loving in the way he waits for me to finish my meal before he gets up *and* clears my plate.

"Izzy is going to drop my mom off at nine, okay?"

"I'll walk with you to the restaurant and run some errands in between."

I don't know what errands I would run at eight o'clock in the morning but I'll make them up if I had to. I just want to walk with him to the restaurant.

When Jordan leaves to get ready in his own apartment, I take a minute to breathe. A lot has changed for me in the last twelve hours. I had sex with another man. I kissed him. I initiated it. *And I liked it.*

***

After spending the morning painting with Jordan's umma, who thoroughly enjoyed the greeting card activity, and kissing Jordan goodbye until tonight, I stepped out into the heat of the early afternoon. April had come and gone in the blink of an eye, and it was already the first week of May.

Spring was in full swing, and my allergies were acting up more than I care for them to. Riding the train gives me a chance to reflect on everything that's happened. I feel guilty about it.

That's what therapy is for, right?

I will get through it. I have to. I'm not about to give up what happiness I've just gotten because my brain can't act right about this situation. I'm not married. I'm not with Gio.

I'm on my own.

I don't know what I can do to convince myself that it's true. For so long, I have acted like I was still with Gio, even when he wasn't here. I knew it would take time to mentally separate us, even though we had been physically separate for so long, but I didn't know how fast I wanted it to happen so I could feel comfortable about being with Jordan.

I'm allowed to see other men. I'm allowed to be happy about it.

Our Lady of Perpetual Help is my oldest and dearest friend now.

Grief can fucking suck it.

Martina welcomes us all in, and I take my usual seat between

Owen and Marcus. Melissa is notably not present for the first time. "Today's topic of group therapy: Practical Considerations," says Martina.

I've been through this type of session at least twice. After our informal introductions, we go around the group and say something that we've been doing that might be seen as impractical, illogical or unhealthy as it relates to our grief—eg: my bags full of Gio's clothes—and other group members then go around and try to come up with seemingly realistic solutions. Except everyone is in the same boat and have all done the same fucked up things at one point or another.

Everyone who has lost a partner is *guaranteed* to have done impractical things like keeping an ancient toothbrush, peeling hairs off an old blanket or left sheets unwashed for months at a time because they still smell like your old love, when in reality it's just your laundry soap.

But sometimes the impractical things are like keeping an old cellphone still in service, or not canceling a magazine subscription or refusing to take a name off a checkbook. As impractical as it is, the little reminders of a person are sometimes what keep you going for so long.

Marcus starts us off. "I'm scared to let Jenny go without water for too long, so I make her take a sip every thirty minutes. I heard that dehydration puts you at risk for a pulmonary embolism, which is what happened to Jessie. I know she's only three years old, and it's unlikely to happen to her, but still, I'm so afraid. I've been struggling to keep my health anxiety in check."

We can all sympathize with Marcus. We tell him, "We're glad you're here," "Thank you for telling us," "Maybe you should talk to your doctor and pediatrician for reassurance."

Adriana tells us how she can't play her wife's favorite CD in the car even though her kids beg her to. She knows it's just a song, but the memories are too strong, and she can't handle them yet. But it's unrealistic to avoid The Beatles forever, especially when her kids love them so much.

"Maybe you should get the kids their own CD player so they can listen on their own, not just in the car with you," suggests Martina. "Rosemary, would you like to go next?"

I think carefully about what I want to say. "I met someone."

A round of hoots and hollers echoes in the church basement.

"I feel so guilty, and I don't know why or what to do. I know I deserve love again. I know I am ready, but I don't know how to get past it."

"Maybe all you need is time to adjust. It might just click for you one day."

"Have you tried talking to your new person about it? He might understand."

"Fake it till you make it, Rosemary."

"Why do you have to stop loving Gio? You can love both of them," Martina tells me.

I don't know what to say. *I can love both of them.*

"I do love both of them, I think."

"Then there you go," says Martina, matter-of-factly. "It is not impractical to devote yourself to someone new, and not to dwell on the past too much."

Martina looks around at the rest of the group and a bunch of ghostly faces stare back at her. "But at the same time, you are allowed to think back fondly on your memories and reserve some of your current and future self to the past. Both of those loves, Rosemary, and both of your selves, can coexist."

"Just don't let it control you," adds Marcus.

Both of my loves can coexist.

You move forward, not on.

"Owen?" Martina continues the group, but I am stuck on what she said to me.

Just as my grieving self is still part of me, Gio will still be part of me, and my guilt will be part of me.

But I won't let it control me. I will learn to love again, in time. In fact, I have been loving again. I am confident that the guilt won't stick with me. I know what I'm doing is right.

I leave the group feeling sure that I can get past this, and with a plan. I will talk to Jordan. I will tell him I love him, and I know I have to be okay with it because that's how I feel, guilty or not.

I am happy, and that's all that matters.

Chapter 18

I leave the church. I'm thrown into the rush of the city, and the more I think about my plan, the more my confidence begins to dwindle. Something about tall buildings makes me feel so small, even though it's us small beings who built them to be so tall. *Is all that matters that I'm happy? What about Jordan?*

Surely he will get sick of my grief sooner or later. And then he'll leave, and I'll be alone again. A person can only take so much crying and hyperventilating and panic.

Every day is the worst day when you're dreading the next.

Even just thinking about telling him I love him makes me want to crawl into a hole and never see the light of day again. Even though it's all I've been thinking about for the last twelve hours.

Even though it *is* true.

Imagine if Gio heard you that love someone else. He'd never forgive you for loving another. Or is it you who'd never forgive yourself?

Imagine if you had to choose. Just like in your dreams. You can only pick one. The dead man or the one who is here. You just have to be brave enough to choose.

Imagine if…

Imagine. And on the train ride home, imagine was all I do.

Different scenarios in which Jordan walks out on me. In the morning. In the afternoon. In the dead of the night, with all his bags packed like a teenage runaway. We'd be fighting after a long night, or he'd get tired of me looking at old photos and memories, and say he'd had enough. He'd leave me all alone again. But still, this is only my second to worst fear.

My worst fear is if his way of walking out is being dead.

I couldn't take another funeral. I couldn't take another casket. I couldn't take another health scare. Not that I wouldn't, but I *couldn't*. There isn't a scenario in which I think I could be okay if Jordan died. He is the first person I've let in since Gio died. Him being gone would crush me in the worst way.

I've already spent so much of my life being sad. I can't spend the next part of whatever is in store for me being sad. The thing about opening yourself up to another person, is that you actually have to stay open. You are not a door. You cannot open and close at will. I love him and I want to be with him, but the vulnerability that comes with it is a thousand knives in my carefully arranged armor. I know I love him. I know I can't do this a second time. The answer was seemingly simple.

I die before him.

Unfortunately, death is not the kind of thing you can arrange.

My mind doesn't know how to grapple with this kind of uncertainty and before I can do the worst and start crying on the subway, I open my phone and text Jordan. I will confess and deal with the repercussions after, self-inflicted or otherwise.

Can you come over before the dinner service? I'll be home in 10.

I'll see you in 20.

It's only 3:10 when I get off the train, so I stop at the corner shop on my way home and pick up real groceries. Apples and carrots and peanut butter fill my basket. On a whim, I purchase a pie crust and as many little limes as I can carry.

I barely lug the stuffed bags into my lobby, my granny cart long forgotten in the corner of my apartment, and unlock my door one handed. Petunia greets me happily, and I'm happy to see her too. I dump my groceries onto my kitchen island and bend down to scratch her head.

I'm startled when my door swings open and Jordan appears in the doorway, dressed in his chef uniform.

"Hey!" He closes the door behind him and crouches down to my eye level. He scritches Petunia lovingly. "How are you? What's up?"

"I'm making dessert." I gesture at the ingredients for a key lime pie piled on my countertop.

We stand and Jordan wraps his arms around my waist. "Good thing. I've been craving a key lime pie and a kiss on the lips." He places a soft kiss on my lips to make his point. "My girlfriend is the best."

I feel the doubt and grief crop up in my chest like seeds in the soil.

Girlfriend. The last time you were somebody's girlfriend, he died. But it wasn't his fault. Cancer doesn't discriminate.

I falter in his arms. What's to say that won't happen now?

"Are you sure you want me to be your girlfriend?" I ask him, doubt riddling my voice like static.

"What?"

"I'm just…" I don't know how to say anything without word vomiting all of my grief, doubt and insecurities. So that's exactly what I do.

"I just am worried one day you'll get sick of my shit and leave me. So maybe it's better we don't label anything."

"Why would I leave you?" Jordan asks, concern anchoring his voice.

"I'm a nervous wreck. I can't remember what my personality is supposed to be. I can't remember who I am anymore, and I feel like an inconvenience to you and the world." Big tears tremble at the edge of my eyelashes. "Look at me, I can't even say I'm your girlfriend without freaking out!"

"Ro, what are you getting at?"

I am already hyperventilating, and it's only been a minute since he walked in.

"Rosemary." Jordan steels me. "Look at me." He gestures his chest upwards, and then downwards. We breathe together, in and out. "Now tell me, what are you worried about?"

"What I'm trying to tell you, is that I want to be your girlfriend. But something about my grief, I can't say it without feeling like I might hyperventilate and have a panic attack. And I don't want you to think that I don't love you because I still have so much grief."

"Ro. I love you and I don't care about your grief. I don't expect it to go away overnight. I've said it before, and I'll say it again, you do what you have to do." Jordan places two hands on my shoulders and before I can look away, my gaze is locked on his eyes.

He loves me.

"Give me a little credit. I won't leave you."

We breathe in harmony while I spill my secrets.

"I'm so scared that one day I'll close my eyes and you'll be gone," I tell him. "I'm so scared you're going to die too. Please don't die, Jordan."

"That is no way to live, Rosemary." Jordan presses a kiss to my forehead and pulls me close to his chest. He puts a hand on my chin and pulls my face to look directly at him. "If I have any say in it, I will not die on you."

"I'm so worried you'll get tired of me loving the two of you."

"I can share with him." He laughs. "I'm not worried about him."

"I'm worried you'll be scared of all my tears."

"Tears don't scare me. I'm not a witch who will melt in the rain." Jordan rubs circles on the small of my back.

"I worry a lot, you know." I bat back my tears. *I will not cry. I will keep it together. I will keep it open.* "It's been a lot for me to do this."

"All your worries are just what if's, Rosemary." He presses a gentle kiss to my cheek. "That is all they will ever be."

Jordan releases me but takes me by the hand and leads me to my sofa. He makes me sit down, and I hang my head like a wilted flower. He kneels and unties my sneakers and removes them from my sore feet. He places Petunia onto my lap, and I hold her like my life depends on it.

"Rosemary. You have nothing to worry about with me. I won't leave. You can count on it."

He places his hands on my knees and waits for me to say something, to do anything.

Worry fills my chest to the brim.

He's just saying that. I am an unbearable human filled with grief. How can I give him the love he deserves with all this grief? How can he be so patient?

"How can you be so understanding?" I ask.

"Because I'm not a terrible fucking human being, Ro. I don't understand where you got this idea that I wouldn't be patient with you." He is earnest and kind.

"From everywhere," I tell him. *Isn't this how it's supposed to be?*

"Forget about everywhere but us."

Jordan himself has only ever shown kindness and compassion towards me. I have no real reason to be afraid he'd leave me. He paid my rent, for god's sake. I don't answer him.

"What would help you be less afraid?" he asks me.

"Time." My voice is shaky and unsure, but I am settled on the answer. *Time is the only thing to help so far.* I'm dumping out the worry in my chest by the bucketful.

"We have all the time in the world." He kisses both my cheeks, my forehead and then my lips, and I let myself be calmed by his touch. "Except, I have to go to prep the dinner service, but I will come back later." Jordan caresses the top of my head before standing.

"I'll be here." I walk him to the door, and before he can leave, I tell him, "Thank you. For everything."

"You know it. You're my girl." We hold hands like lovesick teenagers in the doorway. "You know what? Come by for dinner. I'll cook you something special."

"You sure?"

"Absolutely."

"I'll come at eight." I give a soft smile, all tears seemingly retracted back into my ducts.

As he leaves, for the first time in a long time, I feel at ease.

***

A week later, I arrive at The Red Kettle at approximately 8:00 p.m. It's the first truly warm day of the season, and I have to tie my hair up. My dress sticks to the back of my thighs and before I can regret my outfit choice, Mae is ushering me in and telling me how beautiful I look. She seats me at a table directly in front of the mural.

I admire my work before I sit down. It complements the space quite well, and I'm glad I went with acrylic paints. I snap a photo for my portfolio, not minding the other patrons sitting in front. I spot Jordan in the opposite corner of the restaurant, his hands full of plates, chatting with an older couple.

I take a moment to observe him as he works. He chats with the couple for a few seconds longer before handing dishes off to a busser and moving on to another table. A young couple with a toddler. Hands clasped behind his back, asking them how their food is, he presents them with a grateful smile. Mae walks past him and seemingly whispers something to him, and he turns around towards me.

As Jordan notices me, his grin expands further across his face. He gives me a wave from across the dining room but doesn't make his way over. Instead, he disappears into the kitchen. When he returns, he's carrying a steaming bowl of bulgogi over rice in one hand and a bubbling cup of jasmine tea in the other.

He serves me with a quick kiss on the cheek, before checking in on other customers and then disappearing back into the kitchen, presumably to prepare more meals. I read the specials posted on the wall near the bar—seaweed salad, lollipop chicken, bulgogi and broccoli over rice, crispy tofu tacos and halo halo.

Food is Jordan's love language. He has been feeding me since we met. I think back to the smoothie he made me, the times he fed me after I was painting. The dumplings. How he named his restaurant. It all boiled down to food.

I am fascinated by how much a plate of food says.

Please stay.

You matter to me.

You're home.

I love you.

It isn't the crackers in the cabinet or the key lime pie on the counter that make my house a home. It's the person I'm eating them for. The person I share them with. The whole reason I make the pie in the first place. *I have to tell him.*

As I eat, I design my battle plan. I will stay until closing, and when he comes to walk me home, I will tell him on our doorstep. We'll kiss, and I'll have my happy ending. *I deserve it, after all I've been through.*

I stay at my corner table, watching customers come and go as the hours do, and Jordan flies in and out of the kitchen. He knows the restaurant like the back of his hand. By the time he's finished cleaning, and while I offer to help, he forces me to sit and to draw on some copy paper. It's nearing 10:30 when he finally sits down across from me and lets out a monstrous sigh.

"Long day?" I ask.

"You have no idea."

"It looks really busy. That's good, right?"

"It is, but I'm still exhausted by the end of it." Jordan folds his hands and rests his chin on them. "But you know what would make me feel better?"

"What?" I ask. "Is there anything I can do?"

"A kiss." He points to his lips.

I lean in across the table to place a delicate kiss on his puckered lips. "You smell like fish." *He smells worse than a fish.*

"No kidding." Jordan lets out an uproarious laugh and pulls up his collar to get a whiff. "Yeah, it smells like fish," he confirms.

We look at each other for a beat, our eyes reading one another's faces like words on a page. We say each other's names at the same time.

"You first," he offers, leaning back in his chair.

"I have to tell you something." I say to him, feeling the blush creep up my neck into my ears. *It has to be a dead giveaway.*

"I have to tell you something too."

"Really?" I smile and cross my arms, wondering if it's the same thing I want to tell him. "You first."

He breaks our eye contact and looks away while taking my hand. *Oh, fuck.*

"I sold the apartment."

"*Oh,*" is all I have to say.

"I will close in a month." He holds my hand tighter. "My new apartment is in Grammercy Park. It has three bedrooms. And a beautiful, spacious living room. It's better for my umma. And I won't have to renovate. Your old apartment will still be able to have the original layout Gio designed. And I can put the cabinets back in."

The words are caught in my throat. I don't want him to leave.

"Can we still see each other every day? Grammercy is far."

"Nothing will be closer than two floors above you, Rosemary. But it's not that far."

"It's a train transfer." My heart is caught in my throat.

"It's one train transfer, Ro. I think I can do that much for you. My restaurant is still here, too, you know." Jordan won't look me in the eye. There's something he's not telling me.

"I don't care. You can renovate the apartment. Knock down whatever walls you have to," I say before I can change my mind. I love him, and I don't want him to leave.

"Rosemary," Jordan finally looks me in the face. The corners of his mouth are twisted downward and his eyes tell me everything before he says it. "The housing association won't let me add a third bathroom attached to the bedroom like they initially said. My mother is declining faster than we thought and the halls will not fit a wheelchair." He squeezes my hand tightly. "I have to move for my umma. I hope you understand."

"I understand." I swallow the boulder in my throat. *Don't be an idiot, Rosemary. This isn't about you.* "You do what you have to do, but why wouldn't they let you renovate?"

Jordan swallows his own boulder. "They said a load bearing wall was in need of serious repairs. That the electrical wiring in the apartment should be completely replaced. And that the current work that would need to be done to fix it would take three months. I don't have three months for my umma."

My face falls. I don't remember the apartment being in that much disrepair.

Letters in the mail asking for permission to enter, knocks on the door going unanswered while I was in a puddle on the bathroom floor.

"Why didn't they ask me to make the repairs?" I ask him.

"I don't know." Jordan's face is stone cold sober. "When I asked, they said the landlord wanted to evict the previous tenant over the repairs, but the superintendent convinced him not to and to just raise the rent to an exuberant amount to force them out."

"That's what happened to me." A flurry of anger at Jordan is growing in me, even though this is not even remotely his fault. *I just want to be angry at anyone except myself.* "Is that even legal? How did they let you purchase the apartment?"

"You know how co-op buildings work—and they lowered the asking price if I agreed I would make the repairs myself. The new buyer has agreed to take on the project."

Deleting voicemails asking about the condition of the wall. I didn't want to talk to anyone. I had a home, and I let grief destroy it.

"I'm sorry, Jordan. I didn't mean to let the apartment fall into such disrepair."

"It's not your fault, Ro. The whole section of apartments is facing the same thing." Jordan reassures me. "You were grieving."

"That's not an excuse," I tell him, feeling defeated.

"Yes, it is." Jordan counters. "You lost the love of your life, Rosemary. Give yourself some fucking credit and stop beating yourself up over having grief." His voice hits me like lashes from a whip. "I can't watch you self-depreciate over actual trauma anymore."

What he said echoes around in my head, bouncing around like a pinball.

Give yourself some fucking credit, Rosemary.

When he apologizes for snapping at me, I want to cry again, not because he was too honest and straightforward, but because he's right.

I feel the tension lift from my shoulders and my face. He's right. *He's right.*

Jordan stands up and hauls me to my feet.

"Thank you for standing up for me, for when I couldn't stand up for myself, when the bully was myself," I tell him. "I love you, Jordan." I say the words, dumping out, releasing the worry in my chest by the bucketful. With feeling. With meaning.

Jordan pulls me taut to his chest, and I breathe in his scent despite any fishiness and let myself feel calmed.

"I love you, too, Rosemary," Jordan whispers to the top of my head.

"You really smell like fish." I laugh into his chest, and I know I've got him when he laughs into my hair.

"You mean you're gonna miss it, right?"

"I'll be here every night." I smile into his muscled chest. "As long as you feed me delicious food."

"I'll always cook for you, Ro."

"I knew you loved me," I confess to him.

"How did you know?" I look up at his face as he asks, his stubble growing in slightly, his eyes looking tired from a truly long day.

"The food."

"What do you mean?" I see the puzzlement in his eyes.

"You don't cook food like that for someone you don't love."

"This is my restaurant, Rosemary. I cook like that for everyone."

"You must have a lot of love to give, then," I declare. "Mine tasted especially delicious."

"If you say so."

"I do. I love you."

"I love you, too." Jordan smiles at me.

I am loved, I am loved, I am loved.

Chapter 19

Jordan and I fall into a routine that keeps my heart in balance and time passes for me in a way that it hasn't before. The days morph into one another and the weeks roll past me like subway cars in a station. With ease. Without grief. Every day I look forward to seeing him, and every day I do see him. It is a dream come true for my feeble heart.

In May, we count down the days until June under my bed covers. I meet Jordan at the restaurant at nine every morning and paint with his mother until noon. I go to group therapy and make an effort to participate. We walk home together from The Red Kettle after the dinner service, and I catch up on all the things I've missed in life until it's time to go to sleep.

Nights spent with Jordan are always gone in the blink of an eye, the flap of a firefly's wing, the slamming of a cab door. But he's always back in an instant. He's everywhere I go.

A text message saying good morning.

A note in my paint box.

A leftover meal in my refrigerator.

All the things that made me grieve Gio are all the things that make me love Jordan. I see him in a bouquet of lilies at the corner bodega, a song on the radio, a steaming mug of tea.

In June, I pack up apartment 504 for the second time. All the things that made me sad when I packed it up the first time, make me happy the second time. This time I am not alone. This time it is not goodbye forever. This time is different.

Jordan and I spend two weekends packing up his apartment and moving to his new space, already undergoing renovations. He reminds me with each kiss that this time is different, each brush of his fingertips, each minute he spends listening to me spill my fears. *I am not afraid anymore.*

In July, we find our routine drenched with rolls and rumbles of summer thunderstorms like the ones that drench the city. Eventually, after trial and error and a week apart, we find a new one. I see him every morning to paint with his mother at The Red Kettle, but I spend one weekend at his apartment in Gramercy, he spends the next with me in the West Village. Jordan is both awfully suspicious and excited about his apartment renovations—using tarps to keep me from seeing the final products of his efforts, but at the same time saying, "You'll love it, I promise!"

He fills my apartment with delicious meals and fresh flowers every night. He takes up space in voids I had left empty for so long. I am not afraid to take up his time any longer, either. *I love my new life. I've wanted this for so long, and I've finally let myself have it.* He makes my apartment a home, and Jordan's presence makes me home even when I am by myself.

One hot and humid midsummer evening, we are walking up to Jordan's new building, located in a neighborhood that one could consider an urban forest, the building decorated with an intricate stone facade and a large front stoop. I'm dripping in sweat waiting for Jordan to unlock the vestibule door when he grabs my hand and pulls me towards him into an equally sweaty hug.

"What was that for?" I am disgusted but also pleased with his sudden touch as he slides his hands from my shoulders down to my waist. Even months later, his hands still send electric shocks coursing through my body like an earthquake from an epicenter.

"Just because," he answers, sweat also dripping from his brow, his hands wandering from my waist to the small of my back to my ass.

"That doesn't seem like just because!" I exclaim as he squeezes my butt.

"Actually, there is something I want to talk about."

My face suddenly twists into something crestfallen, confused about what he could want to talk about so suddenly. The night is going well. After dropping Petunia off at her pet hotel, I met him at The Red Kettle at eight, helped him close the restaurant, and made sure to pack a fully stocked overnight bag for a sex-filled and relaxing weekend at his apartment after not seeing each other for more than a few hours in a presentable manner for three days.

"Talk about what?" I ask, but he's still smiling like he didn't just give me a fucking heart attack.

"Come with me." He gives my ass one last squeeze before taking my hand again, totally sweaty, and guiding me up the stairs and into his apartment. We toe off our shoes, and he guides me through the construction zone that is the kitchen and hallway.

The dusty plastic sheet that was formerly covering what would be his new den is finally gone, and instead, I am greeted by…something else.

"What is going on with your living room? Why is there a sink?" I'm confused. There's a large, industrial sink placed in the corner of the room—exactly where I thought he was going to be placing a built-in bookshelf.

"Why do you think, Ro?" Jordan looks at me, excitement sparkling in his eyes, but I'm still not putting two and two together until he hands me a stack of paint brushes that seemingly came out of nowhere.

"You want me to paint in here?"

"It's a studio. For you." He shifts to stand behind me, hugging me from the back. "So you don't have to paint in your living room anymore. We'll move your easels and canvases."

I look around the small room. It's painted a bright shade of light blue with exposed brick on one wall, and has massive, north-facing industrial style windows with what would be tons of natural daylight.

"Why did you do this? What about your den?" I crane my neck to look at him.

"I don't need a den, Ro. I already have the main living room."

Jordan fishes in his gym short pockets for something, and then he hands me a set of keys.

"These are also for you."

I already have keys to his apartment.

"What are these?" *The keys to his heart?*

"The keys to a storage unit."

"A storage unit. A storage unit for what?"

"The unit the cabinets Gio designed are in. And the brass sconces. I saved them, too. They're yours to do with what you want."

"Why would you do this?" I ask, taking the keys from his hands, unsure of what to make of the situation. *I'm so glad he saved them.*

"I know how much they meant to you. I'll install them here, or in your apartment, if you want." Jordan keeps his eyes trained on me, his face beaming. "But I have something else, too."

"Thank you. I'll think about it. I'll definitely use the studio when I am here." I begin to thank him profusely before Jordan cuts me off, taking both my hands in his, his excitement over his next announcement almost too much for his face to bear.

"Rosemary…" He pushes a kiss to my cheek. "Please move in with me and use the studio all of the time."

I knew this was coming. I knew it as soon as he showed me the studio. A man doesn't do all of this and not ask you to move in after. When I don't answer in a heartbeat, he interjects, "You don't have to say yes. Just think about it, please?"

"You don't think it is too soon?" I cock my head, my hair falling to one shoulder.

"I know when it's the right decision."

"What about your umma?" Moving in with Jordan and his mother would certainly prove to be a unique situation.

"She'll be here for a while, of course. She likes you, you know," Jordan answers, squeezing my hands. His umma had a caretaker from mid-morning to mid-evening, who sometimes joined us for painting.

"But if I'm being honest, I think we may have to move her to a round-the-clock monitored facility by the end of the year." Jordan's face is grim. "I can't take care of her the way she needs, with the restaurant. I hope she doesn't deter your decision."

"She doesn't, Jordan." I smile at him. "I didn't even have to think about it. Of course, I will move in with you."

He pulls me into a sweet, mild kiss that quickly turns provocative with the dip and twist of his tongue as he catches his teeth on my bottom lip.

"I can't wait to call this our apartment," he growls into my mouth, his voice low and rapturous.

Just the thought of him kissing me goodnight makes me tingle. Jordan kisses my cheeks and neck like he's doing it for the first time. "I can't wait to see you in our bedroom," I laugh in response to his sudden lack of inhibitions, as his hands make their way to feel up my sides and back. "Whose mattress are we keeping?"

"Yours. I always sleep better on yours." He grumbles into my neck, his hands cupping me, apparently itching to pick me up.

"As long as we can use your sheets and comforter. I can't get enough of how you smell." I inhale a massive breath from his collar bone. "Even when you're disgusting and sweaty."

Jordan's response is to finally pick me up and carry me through the hallway and into his bedroom, soon to be our bedroom, and toss me onto his unmade bed. I laugh maniacally the whole way.

Before I can scold him for tossing me like a magazine, he's on top of me, and kissing me so dearly. He kisses like honey dripping from a spoon, agonizingly tender and slow. I lavish each press of his soft lips with my tongue and my scold is long forgotten.

"Let's give this mattress a good send off, yeah?" Jordan suggests.

"The best send off it could ever imagine," I agree, tugging at his belt loops.

As we undress one another, I am reminded how much physical attention Jordan pays to me. There's always a hand holding mine, or a hand on the small of my back, guiding me through the subway or the grocery store. There's never a moment when we're together that he's not near, reminding me how much he needs me as I need him.

He is eternally anticipating my needs.

"Let me make you come," Jordan whispers. I can hear the hunger in his voice. I lay back on the bed, and he kneels on the floor. He anticipates correctly when he pushes my knees open to kiss down to my thighs and between my legs.

The warmth of his tongue makes my eyes roll back into my head and a groan escapes from my mouth. From a good morning text message to a glass of iced tea to the right kind of tongue flick in bed, he knows me well.

He is never greedy or selfish. He is never impatient or rude. Or, when he is, he is only in the best way. *I love him, I love him, I love him.* And as we move together, I tell him. I pant above his head, my hands wrapped around his shoulders, cradling the back of his head. His bare chest and back is a sight to behold, his tattoos wrapping around the sides of his chest and shoulders.

"I love you back, Rosemary," comes his breathless response.

Each movement of his tongue sets off tiny wildfires inside me. The more he licks, the faster I unravel. "Mostly, I love how you make me come so quickly," I blurt out and laugh in his ear, maybe a little too loud. He makes me come faster than I ever have before. It only takes a good minute.

Jordan's laugh is a literal *ha-ha.*

"You're funny," he coos, climbing out from under me and leaning back on his knees while I prop myself up on my elbows. He wipes my wetness from his mouth before climbing above me to kiss my lips.

He walks around the side of the bed and makes himself comfortable with his back against the wooden headboard and pulls my back to his chest. I can feel the heat radiating off his body like he is the sun, and I can feel him growing harder the more I lean into his pull.

I feel no pressure to initiate or to continue, but after he treats me so well, all I want to do is return the favor. It's always like this. He takes care of me first, then him. As I turn to face him, he's massaging my shoulders, my back, my hips. My bones have never felt so good.

"What do you want, Jordan?" I ask him in a low whisper.

"Anything you'll give me."

I rest on my knees as I hover over him, ready to take him in. He holds my hips steady while I slide over his length, a low groan emitting from somewhere deep in his throat. *Thank god I started birth control last month.* I rock and buck my hips, and when Jordan's eyes flutter closed, I know I've done my job well.

By the time we finish, blue hour is just taking hold, and Jordan's face is more lit by moonlight than by sunshine. He's cradling me in his arms one second and hauling me up the next.

"Paint me something."

"Now?"

"Yes." Jordan pauses for a moment and bats his long eyelashes that no man truly ever deserves to have. "For me?"

With a playful groan, I pull on my panties and T before we make our way through the construction zone that is Jordan's apartment. The place was almost sterile when he moved in, but as more life flows into it, it's becoming something to appreciate. Jordan follows me closely through the apartment to the brand-new studio.

Jordan pulls a small set of acrylic paints and brushes out from under the newly installed sink, and hands me a small 8x10 canvas. I sit cross legged, using the floor as my easel.

"What should I paint?" I ask him, as he sits attentively across from me.

"Anything you want."

"That's always your answer," I say snarkily, recalling how he said that not long ago—in a far different context.

I ponder for a moment. *What does my heart want to paint?* My heart is bursting with a thousand colors, but I only have a meager ten to choose from. I opt for the bright orange. If I am a cool blue, Jordan is a bright orange. His light is never ending, never ceasing. Everything about him screams light and life.

I squeeze a bit of orange, a bit of brown and a bit of green onto my canvas, using it as a mixing palette in a pinch. With the deeper orange, I paint the petals of a tiger lily, and another and another.

With a flick of my wrist, they begin to take form. I slough on the green, mixing it with brown to form the stem.

"How'd you do that so fast?" Jordan asks me, fascinated as I turn the canvas towards him, a single orange lily staring back at him.

"Lots of practice," I tell him, scooching closer, to be cradled in his arms. "I'll teach you one day."

"Promise?" He rests his head on top of mine.

"Promise," I agree. "When I bring my supplies, I fully expect you to learn." I laugh a laugh sweeter than cotton candy.

Before I lose the courage to ask, I sputter out, "Can we install Gio's cabinets here?"

"If that's what you want," Jordan responds, his voice settled.

I look around the apartment, taking in the scene.

The corner unit apartment opens up into the open concept kitchen that looks into the main living room, with the studio space off to the side, enclosed by two French doors. The first hall to the right of the kitchen leads down to the main bedroom with the master bath. The second hall to the left leads to the second and third bedrooms, connected by a jack and jill bathroom, one of which will be used by Jordan's umma.

The kitchen closely resembles Jordan's old kitchen, with many of the same appliances and gadgets and dining room table. His leather sofa sits prominently in the middle of his living room, facing an out-of-commission fireplace with the TV mounted above the mantle. It is very much Jordan's apartment.

And soon it would be mine.

"That's what I want."

Chapter 20

This time I have a choice.

And I choose to tape up the remaining boxes.

I slap packing tape on top of every box with more excitement than I have ever mustered, after putting all of my belongings back into the cardboard boxes and rubber tubs from which they came.

Between all the calamity of packing and moving, I haven't had time to think.

Good fucking riddance is all I have to say this time around. Saying goodbye is usually not an easy task for me, but this time, the words flow off my tongue with ease.

I'm ready to go.

I'm ready and I don't have to convince myself this time.

The first time I walked into this apartment I was a blubbering, miserable mess. But I'm not just a partitioned piece of my old self anymore. I will leave this place a puzzle that is a little bit more put together.

I wasn't anything Jordan did. Love is not a cure—but letting it back into my life, even in the most minuscule of forms—has healed me in the ways I had ached for.

Holding a hand through a balmy walk in the park, basking in the sunshine on a bench.

Watching someone from across the room, knowing you're on their mind.

Placing the last piece of fish on someone else's plate or buying a slice of cake on the way home.

Sharing a bed with a warm body because home is wherever they are.

A home is not the four walls that surround you.

No, I am not miserable any longer. Nothing is out to get me.

It's the kind of summer night where the sky won't let go of the sun, the bars are open till midnight, and everyone is fifteen minutes late because they stop to admire the flowers or pet the stray cat or call their mom. Even though we can't see them, the stars admire us from above.

It's been a month since Jordan asked me to move in, and today, I did. Jordan and I hauled all of my boxes ourselves, and now we sit on the stoop of our building, drinking iced tea straight from the bottle. *This man truly loves me too much. He closed the restaurant for the day to help me.*

Petunia is stretched out on the concrete in front of us. I was more worried about Petunia's adjustment than my own, but she and Umma have become fast friends. Mae and Umma garden in the small terrace in front of the stoop, and soon Jordan will have fresh squashes and peppers and herbs to cook with.

I squeeze Jordan's shoulder, stand up and walk through the vestibule to the apartment door. Gio's cabinets were installed last week. I put my easels in the studio, Petunia's dog beds in the living room, and my crackers in the kitchen cabinet.

I have my own cup of water on the bedside table.

My own mugs in the cabinet.

My shampoo and conditioner in the shower.

But it's my presence in this apartment that makes it mine. For the good and the bad, I'll be here for the memories made within these four walls. As long as this is where Jordan and I are, I'll call this place my home.

I hear quiet footsteps through the entryway as I stand in the kitchen. *That damn love of my life. I've never loved someone the way I love him.*

"What are you thinking, Ro?" he asks, his lanky frame filling the doorway. Jordan's hair has gotten much longer over the summer, and it flops in his face. I'm obsessed with running my hands through it.

My shoes tap along the floor as I walk over to him, my arms reaching out for him, and he automatically wraps me into a hug where I breathe in his scent. *There's something so addictive about him, I can't stop inhaling him.*

"I was just worried about how much I'm not worried." I laugh and look up at him. His brown eyes are alive and sparkling. Jordan's hands travel down to my waist, wrapping behind me.

"There are so many mysteries inside you I'll never understand, Rosemary."

"I'm not worried, for real. I promise." I smile sheepishly and plant a kiss on his cheek before leaning back on the doorframe across from him, and the old hardwood creaks from my weight. "I'm feeling pretty peaceful, actually," I admit.

"You are?" Jordan questions my statement. "What have you done with the real Rosemary?"

"Yeah," I confirm with a grin.

I pause for a minute, to make sure I say what I really want to say.

"I'm happy I'm here," I tell Jordan.

"I'm happy you're here, too," he answers, with a kiss to my temple. He takes my hand and walks me to the stoop, our iced tea sweating on the steps, but I pull him back into the vestibule.

"Jordan."

"Yeah?"

"I love you," I tell him, sincerity covering any fear. "I'm in love with you. I just want you to know I'd choose you a thousand times over. I'll always love Gio, but I would choose you."

"I never doubted you, Rosemary." Jordan's smile is empathetic. *He's always reassuring me without a hint of detesting me.*

"I just had to say it aloud." I'm not going to cry this time, but I preemptively bat my eyes. "I just love you so much." *It makes it more real when I say it.*

"I love you too, Ro."

My heart always melts when he calls me Ro. No one ever called me that before him. I place a kiss so delicately on his lips when he wraps a hand around the back of my head to pull me in closer. I get a taste of his tongue and then he links an arm around mine and pulls me towards the stoop.

"Let's go outside," he whispers into my mouth.

The sun finally melts into the sky, and Jordan's sisters are all arriving for a late dinner. Mae and Umma pet Petunia, Izzie leans on her car parked in the space in front, and Kelly is talking on the phone, sitting on the curb. There's a mountain of cabbage waiting to be turned into kimchi in our refrigerator, and I look forward to Jordan's sisters telling me how I'm doing it all wrong.

Since meeting Jordan, the worst thing I've decided about grief isn't the crying, the lack of intimacy or the paperwork. It's the tearing apart of a family. If it's just the two of you, it tears your family in half, one part never to return.

I had never been close to my parents, and Gio was the only one I could count on for so long. Group therapy had been no replacement.

Meeting Jordan gave me a family back, and I didn't know how

much I needed it until I was sitting on the stoop of a new apartment, watching my dog get loved on, watching two girls bicker over a borrowed sweater, and watching my future mother-in-law count radishes.

I'm still not one to be good with explanations, and lord knows it took me long enough to figure out that grief doesn't have an explanation. It doesn't have to have one.

The fortress around my heart has been knocked and kicked down, not just by Jordan, but by me. By months, years of group therapy. By my own hard work. I took my grief and turned it back in on itself. On the outside, nothing has changed. I paint. I kiss him, and I cry about it.

When does grief turn into guilt? When does guilt turn into punishment?

Guilt is grief. Grief is a testament to how deeply you loved. And if you're lucky, you loved deeply and thoroughly. You don't deserve to be punished for being human.

I don't dream about losing him.

I don't dream about choosing between them.

The two paths of my life that had forked, are now intertwined. Gio's cabinets hold Jordan's pots and pans. Gio's brass sconces light up Jordan's bedroom. *Our bedroom.*

I don't ask myself those questions anymore.

I am the picture-perfect happy family, even on my own. I am everything I used to hate.

A couple, holding hands, laughing in the vegetable aisle of the grocery store.

A woman buying three bouquets of flowers for seemingly no good reason, other than she can.

A normal fucking person who doesn't cry on the train.

I am everything I still hate, too.

I'm sad that Gio doesn't get to experience the things I am now. But his death is not in vain. I live and love because I loved him, and I do because I owe it to myself to make up for the time I spent not letting myself do those things.

Being happy does not negate the grief I felt or will feel, so I should just let myself feel the sunshine on my face, the bustle of the city around me, and the bubbles of joy that appear whenever I look at Jordan.

Now I'm happy, and I let myself be.

Acknowledgements

This book would not be here without many people. Thank you in particular to:

Brendan Reynolds for the cover art and for loving
me unconditionally.

Hayley Shasteen for believing in me from the start.
Gabriel Rios for dying and putting me in this mess
in the first place.

Nora McInerny and The Hot Young Widows
Club for helping me out of this.